SAMUEL TITMARSH
AND THE GREAT
HOGGARTY DIAMOND

W.M. THACKERAY
SAMUEL TITMARSH
AND THE GREAT
HOGGARTY DIAMOND

ALAN SUTTON
1984

Alan Sutton Publishing Limited
Brunswick Road
Gloucester

First published 1841

Copyright © in this edition 1984
Alan Sutton Publishing Limited

British Library Cataloguing in Publication Data

Thackeray, W.M.
   Samuel Titmarsh and the great Hoggarty diamond.
   I. Title
   823'.8[F]   PR5617.53

   ISBN 0-86299-182-X

Cover picture: detail from Mr Roundhand looks out of the Window; *original illustration by W.M. Thackeray, hand tinted by Shelagh Davies*

Typesetting and origination
by Alan Sutton Publishing Limited
Photoset Bembo 9/10
Printed in Great Britain
by The Guernsey Press Company Limited
Guernsey, Channel Islands.

BIOGRAPHICAL NOTE

WILLIAM MAKEPEACE THACKERAY (1811–63). A photograph of Thackeray taken a few years before his death at fifty-two shows him to be a well-dressed hefty man (he was six foot three, and fifteen stone in his forties), with white hair, clean-shaven, with a well-defined mouth, broad-nosed and bespectacled. Behind the spectacles, even in a photograph, the sparkle and depth of his eyes show humour, sadness and insight.

Although Thackeray achieved his ambition of becoming a famous writer, his personal life was one of almost unremitting sadness, relieved only by his loving relationship with his two daughters. His personal experiences and the characters he knew were to be the substance of most of his fictional writing.

He was born in Calcutta, India, on 18 July 1811, the only child of Anne and Richmond Thackeray. The Thackeray family were a well-established Yorkshire family, with branches at Cambridge, and also in India. When William was four, his father died, and his mother married a previous lover, Captain Henry Carmichael-Smyth. Thackeray, meanwhile, was sent to England, to be looked after by his paternal aunt and his maternal grandmother. He went to school at Chiswick Mall, with a disastrous interlude at an inhumane school in Southampton, until his adored mother and respected step-father returned from India in 1820. Then he transferred to Charterhouse, one of the better public schools, but Thackeray was no scholar, and although he was intelligent and ambitious, with a love of reading and the theatre, he showed little persistence in his studies.

This lack of application continued when, after a long break

in Devon at his parents' home, he finally went up to Cambridge, Trinity College. He stayed there for only sixteen months, his good intentions to study being continually shattered by his attraction to lascivious indulgences, including the gambling table, and his unfortunate liaisons with disreputable characters. However, he made his literary debut in *The Snob*, and continued writing for it and its successor, *The Gownsman*, as well as meeting literary men who were to be his friends and acquaintances in the future, among them: Edward Fitzgerald, Tennyson, and William Brookfield. For the next few years, after leaving Cambridge, he lived extravagantly: he spent some months in Weimar, where he met Goethe, fell in love, gambled and learnt German. He then returned to London, and after spending a year deciding not to study law, and then running a literary newspaper at a loss, he retreated to Paris to study art as a poverty-stricken student (since his father's fortune had been mismanaged). Here he met and fell in love with Isabella Shawe. He resolved to marry her in spite of her mother's disapproval, and was pleased to accept the post of French correspondent for *The Constitutional*, a radical newspaper launched with financial assistance from his stepfather. He also produced his first book: *Flore et Zéphyr*, a satire, in 1836, and continued to endeavour to establish himself as an artist.

By July 1837 Thackeray was married to Isabella, a father to baby Annie and unemployed, as *The Constitutional* had folded, and so he was forced to become a freelance journalist, to escape debtor's prison (a situation he explores in *Samuel Titmarsh and the Great Hoggarty Diamond*). He worked as book reviewer, art critic, poet and serial writer for *The Times, Fraser's Magazine*, Dicken's journal *Bentley's Miscellany* and the *New Monthly Magazine*. In 1839 the Thackerays' second daughter died shortly after her birth (another experience relived in *The Great Hoggarty Diamond*), but one year later another girl, Minnie, was born, and Thackeray saw the successful publication of *The Paris Sketch Book*, which received good reviews and interested the important publishing houses of Chapman and Hall, and Longmans. So Thackeray was now an established writer, able to support, if modestly, his young family. However, a happy family life was not to be his, since very soon after the birth of Minnie, Isabella showed the first signs of the madness which was to change her personality, and force Thackeray finally to realise that she would never be cured, and to accept a permanent separation. During these unhappy years he wrote *The History of Samuel Titmarsh and the Great Hoggarty Diamond* (first published in *Bentley's Miscellany*) and then made his first claim to fame as a full length novelist with *Barry Lyndon* (1844). However, the latter was unfavourably received as morally outrageous. In the meantime, he had started to write for *Punch*, and in 1846 he made his first significant impact on Victorian society with his study of English society in *The Snobs of England*. This was followed in 1847 by the first episode of *Vanity Fair*, which was to put Thackeray into the same literary class as the great Dickens, then publishing *Dombey and Son*, and to reintroduce him to the aristocratic circles of London society.

Thackeray had installed his family in a house in Young Street, and was comforted by the memory of the early days of his marriage, his present fame and the company of his daughters. But his heart was lonely for the love of a woman. Consequently he was unable to resist a developing passion for Jane, the young and attractive wife of his old Cambridge friend, William Brookfield. She was Thackeray's 'perfect woman'. He loved her whole-heartedly, and it is this love which pervades *Pendennis*, an autobiographical novel, written 1848–50. But the relationship was doomed since the Brookfields were determined to stay together in spite of their incompatability and finally Thackeray was compelled to break away from both William and Jane. In *The History of Henry Esmond*, completed in 1852 after his separation from the Brookfields, he further explores the emotions of an unhappy marriage, like that of the Brookfields, the frustrated lover and the dominant mother figure. (As an only child, Thackeray was adored and to some extent dominated by his possessive strong-willed mother throughout his whole life.) *Henry Esmond*, set in the early eighteenth century, was his most carefully prepared work: 'Here is the very best I can do . . .', and did not suffer from the fact that Thackeray was seldom at home when he wrote. He had decided, after the publication of *Pendennis* to find another more reliable source of income than writing and had taken up lecturing, a comparatively easy way of making money, and positively lucrative when taken across the Atlantic.

After successful tours in England, he lectured in the States for six months, returning in May 1853, having once again fallen in love, and once again futilely. He knew that Sally Baxter was too young for him. Nevertheless, he was upset by her marriage two years later, and kept in touch with her until her lonely death from tuberculosis in 1862. Sally provided the inspiration for Ethel, the heroine of Thackeray's next novel, *The Newcomes* (1853–5), which again tackled problems of marriage and mothers, and was to be set partly in Rome. To this end, Thackeray took his two daughters to Italy, where he contracted malaria, which was to trouble him for the rest of his life, along with occasional outbreaks of a longstanding and painful bowel condition. It was during his illness in Italy that Thackeray wrote *The Rose and the Ring*, with the close collaboration of a little girl called Edith Story.

When the Thackerays returned to England in 1854 it was to a new house in Onslow Square, with Amy Crowe as companion to Annie and Minnie. Very soon Thackeray was planning a return visit to the States, to lay by some capital for his daughters by giving another lecture tour, this time on the four English King Georges. The expedition was financially successful, but Thackeray was upset by some negative press criticism. However, he came home to deliver the same lectures in England and Scotland. In 1857, with the offer of £6000 for a new serial outstanding, and his name made both as novelist and lecturer, Thackeray made his only stand for Parliament, for the City of Oxford, and was defeated by sixty-five votes. Unsurprised by the result, Thackeray returned to London to concentrate on his next novel, *The Virginians* (1859), which contained English and American characters, and was well received in England and the States.

Thackeray, by now a wealthy man, was able, at the age of forty-nine to achieve his last ambition: to edit his own literary paper. This was the *Cornhill Magazine*, which first appeared in 1860. Contributors included George Eliot, Anthony Trollope, Tennyson and Thackeray himself. He published *The Roundabout Papers*, a notable collection of essays, and his final completed novel: *The Adventures of Philip on his Way Through the*

World. His final extravagant gesture was to rebuild a house, No. 2, Palace Green, Kensington, where he lived for only two years, in decreasing good health, until his death in 1863 from a brain haemorrhage. He was buried in Kensal Green.

SHEILA MICHELL

CHAPTER I.

GIVES AN ACCOUNT OF OUR VILLAGE AND THE FIRST GLIMPSE OF THE DIAMOND

When I came up to town for my second year, my aunt Hoggarty made me a present of a diamond-pin; that is to say, it was not a diamond-pin then, but a large old-fashioned locket, of Dublin manufacture in the year 1795, which the late Mr. Hoggarty used to sport at the Lord Lieutenant's balls and elsewhere. He wore it, he said, at the battle of Vinegar Hill, when his club pigtail saved his head from being taken off, – but that is neither here nor there.

In the middle of the brooch was Hoggarty in the scarlet uniform of the corps of Fencibles to which he belonged; around it were thirteen locks of hair, belonging to a baker's dozen of sisters that the old gentleman had; and, as all these little ringlets partook of the family hue of brilliant auburn, Hoggarty's portrait seemed to the fanciful view like a great fat red round of beef surrounded by thirteen carrots. These were dished up on a plate of blue enamel, and it was from the GREAT HOGGARTY DIAMOND (as we called it in the family,) that the collection of hairs in question seemed as it were to spring.

My aunt, I need not say, is rich; and I thought I might be her heir as well as another. During my month's holiday, she was particularly pleased with me; made me drink tea with her often (though there was a certain person in the village with whom on those golden summer evenings I should have liked to have taken a stroll in the hay-fields); promised every time I drank her bohea to do something handsome for me when I went back to town, – nay, three or four times had me to dinner at three, and to whist or cribbage afterwards. I did not care for the cards; for though we always played seven hours on a stretch, and I always lost, my losings were never more than nineteenpence a night: but there was some infernal sour black-currant wine, that the old lady always produced at dinner, and with the tray at ten o'clock, and which I dared not refuse; though upon my word and honour it made me very unwell.

Well, I thought after all this obsequiousness on my part, and my aunt's repeated promises, that the old lady would at least make me a present of a score of guineas (of which she had a power in the drawer); and so convinced was I that some such present was intended for me, that a young lady by the name of Miss Mary Smith, with whom I had conversed on the subject, actually netted me a little green silk purse, which she gave me (behind Hicks's hayrick, as you turn to the right up Churchyard Lane) – which she gave me, I say, wrapped up in a bit of silver-paper. There was something in the purse, too, if the truth must be known. First, there was a thick curl of the glossiest, blackest hair you ever saw in your life, and next there was threepence: that is to say, the half of a silver sixpence hanging by a little necklace of blue riband. Ah, but I knew where the other half of the sixpence was, and envied that happy bit of silver!

The last day of my holiday I was obliged, of course, to devote to Mrs Hoggarty. My aunt was excessively gracious; and by way of a treat brought out a couple of bottles of the black currant, of which she made me drink the greater part. At night when all the ladies assembled at her party had gone off with their pattens and their maids, Mrs. Hoggarty, who had made a signal to me to stay, first blew out three of the wax-candles in the drawing-room, and taking the fourth in her hand, went and unlocked her escritoire.

I can tell you my heart beat, though I pretended to look quite unconcerned.

'Sam my dear,' said she, as she was fumbling with her keys, 'take another glass of Rosolio' (that was the name by which she baptized the cursed beverage): 'it will do you good.' I took it, and you might have seen my hand tremble as the bottle went click – click against the glass. By the time I had swallowed it, the old lady had finished her operations at the bureau, and was coming towards me, the wax-candle bobbing in one hand and a large parcel in the other.

'Now's the time,' thought I.

'Samuel, my dear nephew,' said she, 'your first name you received from your sainted uncle, my blessed husband; and of all my nephews and nieces, you are the one whose conduct in life has most pleased me.'

When you consider that my aunt herself was one of seven married sisters, that all the Hoggarties were married in Ireland and mothers of numerous children, I must say that the compliment my aunt paid me was a very handsome one.

'Dear aunt,' says I, in a slow, agitated voice, 'I have often heard you say there were seventy-three of us in all, and believe me I do think your high opinion of me very complimentary indeed: I'm unworthy of it – indeed I am.'

'As for those odious Irish people,' says my aunt, rather sharply, 'don't speak of them, I hate them, and every one of their mothers' (the fact is, there had been a lawsuit about Hoggarty's property); 'but of all my other kindred, you, Samuel, have been the most dutiful and affectionate to me. Your employers in London give the best accounts of your regularity and good conduct. Though you have had eighty pounds a year (a liberal salary), you have not spent a shilling more than your income, as other young men would; and you have devoted your month's holidays to your old aunt, who, I assure you, is grateful.'

'Oh, ma'am!' said I. It was all that I could utter.

'Samuel', continued she, 'I promised you a present, and here it is. I first thought of giving you money; but you are a regular lad, and don't want it. You are above money, dear Samuel. I give you what I value most in life – the p, – the po, the po-ortrait of my sainted Hoggarty' (*tears*), 'set in the locket which contains the valuable diamond that you have often heard me speak of. Wear it, dear Sam, for my sake; and think of that angel in heaven, and of your dear aunt Susy.'

She put the machine into my hands: it was about the size of the lid of a shaving-box; and I should as soon have thought of wearing it as of wearing a cocked hat and pigtail. I was so disgusted and disappointed that I really could not get out a single word.

When I recovered my presence of mind a little, I took the locket out of the bit of paper (the locket indeed! it was as big as a barn-door padlock), and slowly put it into my shirt. 'Thank you, aunt,' said I, with admirable raillery. 'I shall always value this present for the sake of you, who gave it me; and it will recall to me my uncle, and my thirteen aunts in Ireland.'

'I don't want you to wear it in *that* way!' shrieked Mrs. Hoggarty, 'with the hair of those odious carroty women. You must have their hair removed.'

'Then the locket will be spoiled, aunt.'

'Well, sir, never mind the locket; have it set afresh.'

'Or suppose,' said I, 'I put aside the setting altogether: it is a little too large for the present fashion; and have the portrait of my uncle framed and placed over my chimney-piece, next to yours. It's a sweet miniature.'

'That miniature,' said Mrs. Hoggarty, solemnly, 'was the great Mulcahy's *chef-d'œuvre*' (pronounced *shy dewver*, a favourite word of my aunt's; being, with the words *bongtong* and *ally mode de Parry*, the extent of her French vocabulary). 'You know the dreadful story of that poor, poor artist. When he had finished that wonderful likeness for the late Mrs. Hoggarty of Castle Hoggarty, county Mayo, she wore it in her bosom at the Lord Lieutenant's ball, where she played a game of piquet with the Commander-in-Chief. What could have made her put the hair of her vulgar daughters round Mick's portrait, I can't think; but so it was, as you see it this day. "Madam," says the Commander-in-Chief, "if that is not my friend Mick Hoggarty, I'm a Dutchman!" Those were his lordship's very words. Mrs Hoggarty of Castle Hoggarty took off the brooch and showed it to him.

'"Who is the artist?" says my lord. "It's the most wonderful likeness I ever saw in my life!"

'"Mulcahy," says she, "of Ormond's Quay."

'"Begad, I patronize him!" says my lord; but presently his face darkened, and he gave back the picture with a dissatisfied air. "There is one fault in that portrait," said his lordship, who was a rigid disciplinarian; "and I wonder that my friend Mick, as a military man, should have overlooked it."

'"What's that?" says Mrs. Hoggarty of Castle Hoggarty.

'"Madam, he has been painted WITHOUT HIS SWORD-BELT!" and he took up the cards again in a passion, and finished the game without saying a single word.

'The news was carried to Mr. Mulcahy the next day, and that unfortunate artist *went mad immediately*! He had set his whole reputation upon this miniature, and declared that it should be faultless. Such was the effect of the announcement upon his susceptible heart! When Mrs. Hoggarty died, your uncle took the portrait and always wore it himself. His sisters said it was for the sake of the diamond; whereas, ungrateful things! it was merely on account of their hair, and his love for the fine arts. As for the poor artist, my dear, some people said it was the profuse use of spirit that brought on delirium tremens; but I don't believe it. Take another glass of Rosolio.'

The telling of this story always put my aunt into great good-humour, and she promised at the end of it to pay for the new setting of the diamond; desiring me to take it on my arrival in London to the great jeweller, Mr. Polonius, and send her the bill. 'The fact is,' said she, 'that the gold in which the thing is set is worth five guineas at the very least, and you can have the diamond reset for two. However, keep the remainder, dear Sam, and buy yourself what you please with it.'

With this the old lady bade me adieu. The clock was striking twelve as I walked down the village, for the story of Mulcahy always took an hour in the telling, and I went away not quite so down-hearted as when the present was first made to me. 'After all,' thought I, 'a diamond-pin is a handsome thing, and will give me a *distingué* air, though my clothes be never so shabby' – and shabby they were without any doubt. 'Well,' I said, 'three guineas, which I shall have over, will buy me a couple of pairs of what-d'ye-call-'ems;' of which, *entre nous*, I was in great want, having just then done growing, whereas my pantaloons were made a good eighteen months before.

Well, I walked down the village, my hands in my breeches-pockets; I had poor Mary's purse there, having removed the little things which she gave me the day before, and placed them – never mind where: but look you, in those days I had a heart, and a warm one too. I had Mary's purse ready for my aunt's donation, which never came, and with my own little stock of money besides, that Mrs. Hoggarty's card-parties had lessened by a good five-and-twenty shillings, I calculated that, after paying my fare, I should get to town with a couple of seven-shilling pieces in my pocket.

I walked down the village at a deuce of a pace; so quick that, if the thing had been possible, I should have overtaken ten o'clock that had been passed by me two hours ago, when I was listening to Mrs. H.'s long stories over her terrible Rosolio. The truth is, at ten I had an appointment under a certain person's window, who was to have been looking at the moon at that hour, with her pretty quilled nightcap on, and her blessed hair in papers.

There was the window shut, and not so much as a candle in it; and though I hemmed and hawed, and whistled over the garden-paling, and sang a song of which Somebody was very fond, and even threw a pebble at the window, which hit it exactly at the opening of the lattice, – I woke no one except a great brute of a house-dog, that yelled, and howled, and bounced so at me over the rails, that I thought every moment he would have had my nose between his teeth.

So I was obliged to go off as quickly as might be; and the next morning mamma and my sisters made breakfast for me at four, and at five came the True Blue light six-inside post-coach to London, and I got up on the roof without having seen Mary Smith.

As we passed the house, it *did* seem as if the window-curtain in her room was drawn aside just a little bit. Certainly the window was open, and it had been shut the night before: but away went the coach; and the village, cottage, and the churchyard, and Hicks's hayricks, were soon out of sight.

'My hi, what a pin!' said a stable-boy, who was smoking a cigar, to the guard, looking at me and putting his finger to his nose.

The fact is, that I had never undressed since my aunt's party; and being uneasy in mind, and having all my clothes to pack up, and thinking of something else, had quite forgotten Mrs. Hoggarty's brooch, which I had stuck into my shirt-frill the night before.

CHAPTER II.

TELLS HOW THE DIAMOND IS BROUGHT UP TO LONDON, AND PRODUCES WONDERFUL EFFECTS BOTH IN THE CITY AND AT THE WEST END

The circumstances recorded in this story took place some score of years ago, when, as the reader may remember, there was a great mania in the city of London for establishing companies of all sorts; by which many people made pretty fortunes.

I was at this period, as the truth must be known, thirteenth clerk of twenty-four young gents who did the immense business of the Independent West Diddlesex Fire and Life Insurance Company, at their splendid stone mansion in Cornhill. Mamma had sunk a sum of four hundred pounds in the purchase of an annuity at this office, which paid her no less than six-and thirty pounds a year, when no other company in London would give her more than twenty-four. The chairman of the directors was the great Mr. Brough, of the house of Brough and Hoff, Crutched Friars, Turkey Merchants. It was a new house, but did a tremendous business in the fig and sponge way, and more in the Zante currant line than any other firm in the city.

Brough was a great man among the Dissenting connection, and you saw his name for hundreds at the head of every charitable society patronized by those good people. He had nine clerks residing at his office in Crutched Friars; he would not take one without a certificate from the schoolmaster and clergyman of his native place, strongly vouching for his morals and doctrine; and the places were so run after, that he got a premium of four or five hundred pounds with each young gent, whom he made to slave for ten hours a day, and to whom in compensation he taught all the mysteries of the Turkish business. He was a great man on 'Change, too; and our young chaps used to hear from the stockbrokers' clerks (we commonly dined together at the 'Cock and Woolpack,' a respectable house, where you get a capital cut of meat, bread, vegetables, cheese, half a pint of porter, and a penny to the waiter, for a shilling) – the young stockbrokers used to tell us of immense bargains in Spanish, Greek, and Columbians, that Brough made. Hoff had nothing to do with them, but stopped at home minding exclusively the business of the house. He was a young chap, very quiet and steady, of the Quaker persuasion, and had been taken into partnership by Brough for a matter of thirty thousand pounds: and a very good bargain too. I was told in the strictest confidence that the house one year with another divided a good seven thousand pounds; of which Brough had half, Hoff, two sixths, and the other sixth went to old Tudlow, who had been Mr. Brough's clerk before the new partnership began. Tudlow always went about very shabby, and we thought him an old miser. One of our gents, Bob Swinney by name, used to say that Tudlow's share was all nonsense, and that Brough had it all; but Bob was always too knowing by half, used to wear a green cut-away coat, and had his free admission to Covent Garden theatre. He was always talking down at the shop, as we called it (it wasn't a shop, but as splendid an office as any in Cornhill) – he was always talking about Vestris and Miss Tree, and singing,

> 'The bramble, the bramble,
> The jolly, jolly bramble!'

one of Charles Kemble's famous songs in 'Maid Marian;' a play that was all the rage then, taken from a famous story-book by one Peacock, a clerk in the India House: and a precious good place he has too.

When Brough heard how Master Swinney abused him, and had his admission to the theatre, he came one day down to the office where we all were, four-and-twenty of us, and made one of the most beautiful speeches I ever heard in my life. He said that for slander he did not care, contumely was the lot of every public man who had austere principles of his own, and acted by them austerely; but what he *did* care for was the character of every single gentleman forming a part of the Independent West Diddlesex Association. The welfare of thousands was in their keeping; millions of money were daily passing through their hands; the city – the country looked upon them for order, honesty, and good example. And if he found amongst those whom he considered as his children – those whom he loved as his own flesh and blood – that that order was departed from, that that regularity was not maintained, that that good example was not kept up (Mr. B. always spoke in this emphatic way) – if he found his children departing from the wholesome rules of morality, religion, and decorum – if he found in high or low – in the head clerk at six hundred a year down to the porter who cleaned the steps – if he found the slightest taint of dissipation, he would cast the offender from him – yea, though he were his own son, he would cast him from him!

As he spoke this, Mr. Brough burst into tears; and we who didn't know what was coming, looked at each other as pale as parsnips: all except Swinney, who was twelfth clerk, and made believe to whistle. When Mr. B. had wiped his eyes and recovered himself, he turned round; and oh, how my heart thumped as he looked me full in the face! How it was relieved, though, when he shouted out in a thundering voice, –

'Mr. ROBERT SWINNEY!'

'Sir to you,' says Swinney, as cool as possible, and some of the chaps began to titter.

'Mr. SWINNEY!' roared Brough, in a voice still bigger than before, 'when you came into this office – this family, sir, for such it is, as I am proud to say – you found three-and-twenty as pious and well-regulated young men as ever laboured together – as ever had confided to them the wealth of this mighty capital and famous empire. You found, sir, sobriety, regularity, and decorum; no profane songs were uttered in this place sacred to – to business; no slanders were whispered against the heads of the establishment – but over them I pass: I can afford, sir, to pass them by – no worldly conversation or foul jesting disturbed the attention of these gentlemen, or desecrated the peaceful scene of their labours. You found Christians and gentlemen, sir!'

'I paid for my place like the rest,' said Swinney. 'Didn't my governor take sha— ?'

'Silence, sir! Your worthy father did take shares in this establishment, which will yield him one day an immense profit. He *did* take shares, sir, or you never would have been here. I glory in saying that every one of my young friends around me has a father, a brother, a dear relative or friend, who is connected in a similar way with our glorious enterprise; and that not one of them is there but has an interest in procuring, at a liberal commission, other persons to join the ranks of our association. *But*, sir, I am its chief. You will find, sir, your appointment signed by me; and in like manner, I, John Brough, annul it. Go from us sir! – leave us – quit a family that can no longer receive you in its bosom! Mr. Swinney, I have wept, I have prayed, sir, before I came to this determination; I have taken counsel, sir, and am resolved. *Depart from out of us!*'

'Not without three months' salary, though, Mr. B.: that cock won't fight!'

'They shall be paid to your father, sir.'

'My father be hanged! I'll tell you what, Brough, I'm of age; and if you don't pay me my salary, I'll arrest you, – by jingo, I will! I'll have you in quod, or my name's not Bob Swinney!'

'Make out a cheque, Mr. Roundhand, for the three months' salary of this perverted young man.'

'Twenty-one pun' five, Roundhand, and nothing for the stamp!' cried out that audacious Swinney. 'There it is, sir, *re-*ceipted. You needn't cross it to my banker's. And if any of you gents like a glass of punch this evening at eight o'clock, Bob Swinney's your man, and nothing to pay. If Mr. Brough *would* do me the honour to come in and take a whack? Come, don't say no, if you'd rather not!'

We couldn't stand this impudence, and all burst out laughing like mad.

'Leave the room!' yelled Mr. Brough, whose face had turned quite blue; and so Bob took his white hat off the peg, and strolled away with his 'tile,' as he called it, very much on one side. When he was gone, Mr. Brough gave us another lecture, by which we all determined to profit; and going up to Roundhand's desk put his arm round his neck, and looked over the ledger.

'What money has been paid in to-day, Roundhand?' he said, in a very kind way.

'The widow, sir, came with her money: nine hundred and four ten and six – say 904*l*. 10*s*. 6*d*. Captain Sparr, sir, paid his shares up; grumbles, though, and says he's no more: fifty shares – two instalments – three fifties, sir.'

'He's always grumbling!'

'He says he has not a shilling to bless himself with until our dividend day.'

'Any more?'

Mr Roundhand went through the book, and made it up nineteen hundred pounds in all. We were doing a famous business now; though when I came into the office we used to sit and laugh, and joke, and read the newspapers all day; bustling into our seats whenever a stray customer came. Brough never cared about our laughing and singing *then*, and was hand and glove with Bob Swinney; but that was in early times, before we were well in harness.

'Nineteen hundred pounds, and a thousand pounds in shares. Bravo, Roundhand – bravo, gentlemen! Remember, every share you bring in brings you five per cent. down on the nail! Look to your friends – stick to your desks – be regular – I hope none of you forget church. Who takes Mr. Swinney's place?'

'Mr Samuel Titmarsh, sir.'

'Mr. Titmarsh, I congratulate you. Give me your hand, sir: you are now twelfth clerk of this Association, and your salary is consequently increased five pounds a year. How is your worthy mother, sir – your dear and excellent parent? In good health, I trust? And long – long, I fervently pray, may this office continue to pay her annuity! Remember, if she has more money to lay out, there is higher interest than the last for her, for she is a year older; and five per cent. for you, my boy! Why not you as well as another? Young men will be young men, and a ten-pound note does no harm. Does it, Mr. Abednego?'

'Oh, no!' says Abednego, who was third clerk, and who was the chap that informed against Swinney; and he began to laugh, as indeed we all did whenever Mr. Brough made anything like a joke: not that they *were* jokes; only we used to know it by his face.

'Oh, by-the-by, Roundhand,' says he, 'a word with you on business. Mrs. Brough wants to know why the deuce you never come down to Fulham?'

'Law, that's very polite!' said Mr. Roundhand, quite pleased.

'Name your day, my boy! Say Saturday, and bring your nightcap with you.'

'You're very polite, I'm sure. I should be delighted beyond anything, but – '

'But – no buts, my boy! Hark ye! the Chancellor of the Exchequer does me the honour to dine with us, and I want you to see him; for the truth is, I have bragged about you to his lordship as the best actuary in the three kingdoms.'

Roundhand could not refuse such an invitation as *that*, though he had told us how Mrs. R. and he were going to pass Saturday and Sunday at Putney; and we who knew what a life the poor fellow led, were sure that the head clerk would be prettily scolded by his lady when she heard what was going on. She disliked Mrs. Brough very much, that was the fact; because Mrs. B. kept a carriage, and said she didn't know where Pentonville was, and couldn't call on Mrs. Roundhand. Though, to be sure, her coachman might have found out the way.

'And oh, Roundhand!' continued our governor, 'draw a cheque for seven hundred, will you? Come, don't stare, man; I'm not going to run away! That's right, – seven hundred – and ninety say, while you're about it! Our board meets on Saturday, and never fear I'll account for it to them before I drive you down. We shall take up the Chancellor at White-hall.'

So saying, Mr. Brough folded up the cheque, and shaking hands with Mr. Roundhand very cordially, got into his carriage-and-four (he always drove four horses even in the city, where it's so difficult), which was waiting at the office-door for him.

Bob Swinney used to say that he charged two of the horses to the company; but there was never believing half of what that Bob said, he used to laugh and joke so. I don't know how it was, but I and a gent by the name of Hoskins (eleventh clerk), who lived together with me in Salisbury Square, Fleet Street – where we occupied a very genteel two-pair – found our flute duet rather tiresome that evening, and as it was a very fine night, strolled out for a walk West End way. When we arrived opposite 'Covent Garden Theatre' we found ourselves close to the 'Globe Tavern,' and recollected Bob Swinney's hospitable invitation. We never fancied that he had meant the invitation in earnest, but thought we might as well look in: at any rate there could be no harm in doing so.

There, to be sure, in the back drawing-room, where he said he would be, we found Bob at the head of a table, and in the midst of a great smoke of cigars, and eighteen of our gents rattling and banging away at the table with the bottoms of their glasses.

What a shout they made as we came in! 'Hurray!' says Bob, 'here's two more! Two more chairs, Mary, two more tumblers, two more hot waters, and two more goes of gin! Who would have thought of seeing Tit, in the name of goodness?'

'Why,' said I, 'we only came in by the merest chance.'

At this word there was another tremendous roar: and it is a positive fact, that every man of the eighteen had said he came by chance! However, chance gave us a very jovial night; and that hospitable Bob Swinney paid every shilling of the score.

'Gentlemen!' says he, as he paid the bill, 'I'll give you the health of John Brough, Esquire, and thanks to him for the present of 21l. 5s. which he made me this morning. What do I say – 21l. 5s? That and a month's salary that I should have had to pay – forfeit – down on the nail, by jingo! for leaving the shop, as I intended to do to-morrow morning. I've got a place – a tip-top place, I tell you. Five guineas a week, six journeys a year, my own horse, and gig, and to travel in the West of England in oil and spermaceti. Here's confusion to gas, and the health of Messrs. Gann and Co., of Thames Street, in the city of London!'

I have been thus particular in my account of the West Diddlesex Assurance Office, and of Mr. Brough, the managing director (though the real names are neither given to the office nor to the chairman, as you may be sure), because the fate of me and my diamond-pin was mysteriously bound up with both: as I am about to show.

You must know that I was rather respected among our gents at the West Diddlesex, because I came of a better family than most of them; had received a classical education; and especially because I had a rich aunt, Mrs. Hoggarty, about whom, as must be confessed, I used to boast a good deal. There is no harm in being respected in this world, as I have found out; and if you don't brag a little for yourself, depend on it there is no person of your acquaintance who will tell the world of your merits, and take the trouble off your hands.

So that when I came back to the office after my visit at home, and took my seat at the old day-book opposite the dingy window that looks into Birchin Lane, I pretty soon let the fellows know that Mrs. Hoggarty, though she had not given me a large sum of money, as I expected – indeed, I had promised a dozen of them a treat down the river, should the promised riches have come to me – I let them know, I say, that though my aunt had not given me any money, she had given me a splendid diamond, worth at least thirty guineas, and that some day I would sport it at the shop.

'Oh, let's see it!' says Abednego, whose father was a mock-jewel and gold-lace merchant in Hanway Yard; and I promised that he should have a sight of it as soon as it was set. As my pocket-money was run out too (by coach-hire to and from home, five shillings to our maid at home, ten to my aunt's maid and man, five-and-twenty shillings lost at whist, as I said, and fifteen-and-six paid for a silver scissors for the dear little fingers of Somebody), Roundhand, who was very good-natured, asked me to dine, and advanced me 7l. 1s. 8d., a month's salary. It was at Roundhand's house, Myddelton Square, Pentonville, over a fillet of veal and bacon and a glass of port, that I learned and saw how his wife ill-treated him; as I have told before. Poor fellow! – we under-clerks all thought it was a fine thing to sit at a desk by oneself, and have 50l. per month, as Roundhand had; but I've a notion that Hoskins and I, blowing duets on the flute together in our second floor in Salisbury Square, were a great deal more at ease than our head – and more *in harmony*, too; though we made sad work of the music, certainly.

One day Gus Hoskins and I asked leave from Roundhand to be off at three o'clock, as we had *particular business* at the West End. He knew it was about the great Hoggarty diamond, and gave us permission; so off we set. When we reached St. Martin's Lane, Gus got a cigar, to give himself as it were a *distingue´* air, and puffed at it all the way up the Lane, and through the alleys into Coventry Street, where Mr. Polonius's shop is, as everybody knows.

The door was open, and a number of carriages full of ladies were drawing up and setting down. Gus kept his hands in his pockets – trousers were worn very full then, with large tucks, and pigeon-holes for your boots, or Bluchers, to come through (the fashionables wore boots, but we chaps in the city, on 80*l.* a year, contented ourselves with Bluchers); and as Gus stretched out his pantaloons as wide as he could from his hips, and kept blowing away at his cheroot, and clamping with the iron heels of his boots, and had very large whiskers for so young a man, he really looked quite the genteel thing, and was taken by everybody to be a person of consideration.

He would not come into the shop though, but stood staring at the gold pots and kettles in the window outside. I went in; and after a little hemming and hawing – for I had never been at such a fashionable place before – asked one of the gentlemen to let me speak to Mr. Polonius.

'What can I do for you, sir?' says Mr. Polonius, who was standing close by, as it happened, serving three ladies, – a very old one and two young ones, who were examining pearl-necklaces very attentively.

'Sir,' said I, producing my jewel out of my coat-pocket, 'this jewel has, I believe, been in your house before: it belonged to my aunt, Mrs. Hoggarty, of Castle Hoggarty.' The old lady standing near looked round as I spoke.

'I sold her a gold neck-chain and repeating watch in the year 1795,' said Mr. Polonius, who made it a point to recollect everything; 'and a silver punch-ladle to the captain. How is the major – colonel – general – ay, sir?'

'The general,' said I, 'I am sorry to say' – though I was quite proud that this man of fashion should address me so – 'Mr. Hoggarty is – no more. My aunt has made me a present, however, of this – this trinket – which, as you see, contains her husband's portrait, that I will thank you, sir, to preserve for me very carefully; and she wishes that you would set this diamond neatly.'

'Neatly and handsomely of course, sir.'

'Neatly, in the present fashion; and send down the account to her. There is a great deal of gold about the trinket, for which, of course, you will make an allowance.'

'To the last fraction of a sixpence,' says Mr. Polonius, bowing, and looking at the jewel. 'It's a wonderful piece of goods, certainly,' said he; 'though the diamond's a neat little bit, certainly. Do, my lady, look at it. The thing is of Irish manufacture, bears the stamp of '95, and will recall perhaps the times of your ladyship's earliest youth.'

'Get ye out, Mr. Polonius!' said the old lady, a little wizen-faced old lady, with her face puckered up in a million of wrinkles. 'How *dar* you, sir, to talk such nonsense to an old woman like me? Wasn't I fifty years old in '95, and a grandmother in '96?' She put out a pair of withered, trembling hands, took up the locket, examined it for a minute, and then burst out laughing. 'As I live, it's the great Hoggarty diamond!'

Good heavens! what was this talisman that had come into my possession?

'Look, girls,' continued the old lady: 'this is the great jew'l of all Ireland. This red-faced man in the middle is poor Mick Hoggarty, a cousin of mine, who was in love with me in the year '84, when I had just lost your poor dear grandpapa. These thirteen sthreamers of red hair represent his thirteen celebrated sisters, – Biddy, Minny, Thedy, Widdy (short for Williamina), Freddy, Izzy, Tizzy, Mysie, Grizzy, Polly, Dolly, Nell, and Bell – all married, all ugly, and all carr'ty hair. And of which are you the son, young man? – though, to do you justice, you're not like the family.'

Two pretty young ladies turned two pretty pairs of black eyes at me, and waited for an answer: which they would have had, only the old lady began rattling on a hundred stories about the thirteen ladies above named, and all their lovers, all their disappointments, and all the duels of Mick Hoggarty. She was a chronicle of fifty-years-old scandal. At last she was interrupted by a violent fit of coughing; at the conclusion of which Mr. Polonius very respectfully asked me where he should send the pin, and whether I would like the hair kept.

'No,' says I, 'never mind the hair.'

'And the pin, sir?'

I had felt ashamed about telling my address: 'But, hang it!'
thought I, 'why *should* I? –

> 'A king can make a belted knight,
>   A marquess, duke, and a' that;
> An honest man's abune his might –
>   Gude faith, he canna fa' that.'

Why need I care about telling these ladies where I live?'

'Sir,' says I, 'have the goodness to send the parcel, when
done, to Mr. Titmarsh, No. 3, Bell Lane, Salisbury Square,
near St. Bride's Church, Fleet Street. Ring, if you please, the
two-pair bell.'

'*What*, sir?' said Mr. Polonius.

'*Hwat!*' shrieked the old lady. 'Mr. Hwat? *Mais, ma chère,
c'est impayable.* Come along – here's the carr'age? Give me
your arm, Mr. Hwat, and get inside, and tell me all about
your thirteen aunts.'

She seized on my elbow and hobbled through the shop as
fast as possible; the young ladies following her, laughing.

'Now, jump in, do you hear?' said she, poking her sharp
nose out of the window.

'I can't, ma'am,' says I; 'I have a friend.'

'Pooh, pooh! send 'um to the juice, and jump in!' And
before almost I could say a word, a great powder'd fellow in
yellow-plush breeches pushed me up the steps and banged the
door to.

I looked just for one minute as the barouche drove away at
Hoskins, and never shall forget his figure. There stood Gus,
his mouth wide open, his eyes staring, a smoking cheroot in
his hand, wondering with all his might at the strange thing
that had just happened to me.

'Who *is* that Titmarsh?' says Gus: 'there's a coronet on the
carriage, by jingo!'

CHAPTER III

HOW THE POSSESSOR OF THE DIAMOND IS WHISKED INTO A MAGNIFICENT CHARIOT, AND HAS YET FURTHER GOOD LUCK

I sat on the back seat of the carriage, near a very nice young lady, about my dear Mary's age – that is to say, seventeen and three quarters; and opposite us sat the old countess and her other grand-daughter – handsome too, but ten years older. I recollect I had on that day my blue coat and brass buttons, nankeen trousers, a white sprig waistcoat, and one of Dando's silk hats, that had just come in the year '22, and looked a great deal more glossy than the best beaver.

'And who was that hidjus manster' – that was the way her ladyship pronounced, – 'that ojous vulgar wretch, with the iron heels to his boots, and the big mouth, and the imitation goold neck chain, who *steered* at us so as we got into the carr'age?'

How she should have known that Gus's chain was mosaic I can't tell; but so it was, and we had bought it for five-and-twenty and sixpence only the week before at M'Phail's, in St. Paul's Churchyard. But I did not like to hear my friend abused, and so spoke out for him, –

'Ma'am,' says I, 'that young gentleman's name is Augustus Hoskins. We live together; and a better or more kind-hearted fellow does not exist.'

'You are quite right to stand up for your friends, sir,' said the second lady; whose name, it appears, was Lady Jane, but whom the grandmamma called Lady Jene.

'Well, upon me canscience, so he is now, Lady Jene; and I like sper't in a young man. So his name is Hoskins, is it? I know, my dears, all the Hoskinses in England. There are the Lincolnshire Hoskinses, the Shropshire Hoskinses: they say the admiral's daughter, Bell, was in love with a black footman, or boatswain, or some such thing; but the world's so censorious. There's old Doctor Hoskins of Bath, who attended poor dear Drum in the quinsy; and poor dear old Fred Hoskins, the gouty general: I remember him as thin as a lath in the year '84, and as active as a harlequin, and in love with me – oh, how he was in love with me!'

'You seem to have had a host of admirers in those days, grandmamma?' said Lady Jane.

'Hundreds, my dear, – hundreds of thousands. I was the toast of Bath, and a great beauty, too: would you ever have thought it now, upon your conscience and without flattery, Mr.-a-What-d'ye-call-'im?'

'Indeed, ma'am, I never should,' I answered, for the old lady was as ugly as possible; and at my saying this the two young ladies began screaming with laughter, and I saw the two great-whiskered footmen grinning over the back of the carriage.

'Upon my word, you're mighty candid, Mr. What's-your-name – mighty candid indeed; but I like candour in young people. But a beauty I was. Just ask your friend's uncle the general. He's one of the Lincolnshire Hoskinses – I knew he was by the strong family likeness. Is he the eldest son? It's a pretty property, though sadly encumbered; for old Sir George was the divvle of a man – a friend of Hanbury Williams, and Lyttleton, and those horrid, monstrous, ojous people! How much will he have now, mister, when the admiral dies?'

'Why, ma'am, I can't say; but the admiral is not my friend's father.'

'Not his father? – but he *is*, I tell you, and I'm never wrong. Who is his father, then?'

'Ma'am, Gus's father's a leather-seller in Skinner Street, Snow Hill, – a very respectable house, ma'am. But Gus is only third son, and so can't expect a great share in the property.'

The two young ladies smiled at this – the old lady said, 'Hwat?'

'I like you, sir,' Lady Jane said, 'for not being ashamed of your friend, whatever their rank of life may be. Shall we have the pleasure of setting you down anywhere, Mr. Titmarsh?'

'Noways particular, my lady,' says I. 'We have a holiday at our office to-day – at least Roundhand gave me and Gus leave; and I shall be very happy, indeed, to take a drive in the Park, if it's no offence.'

'I'm sure it will give us – infinite pleasure,' said Lady Jane; though rather in a grave way.

'Oh, that it will!' says Lady Fanny, clapping her hands: 'won't it, grandmamma? And after we have been in the Park, we can walk in Kensington Gardens, if Mr. Titmarsh will be good enough to accompany us.'

'Indeed, Fanny, we will do no such thing,' says Lady Jane.

'Indeed but we will though!' shrieked out Lady Drum. 'Ain't I dying to know everything about his uncle and thirteen aunts? and you're all chattering so, you young women, that not a blessed syllable will you allow me or my young friend here to speak.'

Lady Jane gave a shrug with her shoulders, and did not say a single word more. Lady Fanny, who was as gay as a young kitten (if I may be so allowed to speak of the aristocracy), laughed, and blushed, and giggled, and seemed quite to enjoy her sister's ill humour. And the countess began at once, and entered into the history of the thirteen Misses Hoggarty, which was not near finished when we entered the Park.

When there, you can't think what hundreds of gents on horseback came to the carriage and talked to the ladies. They had their joke for Lady Drum, who seemed to be a character in her way; their bow for Lady Jane; and, the young ones especially, their compliment for Lady Fanny.

Though she bowed and blushed, as a young lady should, Lady Fanny seemed to be thinking of something else; for she kept her head out of the carriage, looking eagerly among the horsemen, as if she expected to see somebody. Aha! my Lady Fanny, *I* knew what it meant when a young, pretty lady like you was absent, and on the look-out, and only half answered the questions put to her. Let alone Sam Titmarsh – he knows what *somebody* means as well as another, I warrant. As I saw these manœuvres going on, I could not help just giving a wink to Lady Jane, as much as to say I knew what was what. 'I guess the young lady is looking for Somebody,' says I. It was then *her* turn to look queer, I assure you, and she blushed as red as scarlet, but, after a minute, the good-natured little thing looked at her sister, and both the young ladies put their handkerchiefs up to their faces, and began laughing – laughing as if I had said the funniest thing in the world.

'*Il est charmant, votre monsieur,*' said Lady Jane to her grandmamma; and on which I bowed and said, '*Madame, vous me faites beaucoup d'honneur:*' for I know the French language, and was pleased to find that these good ladies had taken a liking to me. 'I'm a poor humble lad, ma'am, not used to London society, and do really feel it quite kind of you to take me by the hand so, and give me a drive in your fine carriage.'

At this minute a gentleman on a black horse, with a pale face and a tuft to his chin, came riding up to the carriage; and I knew by a little start that Lady Fanny gave, and by her instantly looking round the other way, that *Somebody* was come at last.

'Lady Drum,' said he, 'your most devoted servant! I have just been riding with a gentleman who almost shot himself for love of the beautiful Countess of Drum in the year – never mind the year.'

'Was it Killblazes?' said the lady: 'he's a dear old man, and I'm quite ready to go off with him this minute. Or was it that delight of an old bishop? He's got a lock of my hair now – I gave it him when he was papa's chaplain; and let me tell you it would be a hard matter to find another now in the same place.'

'Law, my lady!' says I, 'you don't say so?'

'But indeed I do, my good sir,' says she; 'for between ourselves, my head's as bare as a cannon-ball – ask Fanny if it isn't. Such a fright as the poor thing got when she was a babby, and came upon me suddenly in my dressing-room without my wig!'

'I hope Lady Fanny has recovered from the shock,' said 'Somebody,' looking first at her, and then at me as if he had a mind to swallow me. And would you believe it? all that Lady Fanny could say was, 'Pretty well, I thank you, my lord;' and she said this with as much fluttering and blushing as we used to say our Virgil at school – when we hadn't learned it.

My lord still kept on looking very fiercely at me, and muttered something about having hoped to find a seat in Lady

Drum's carriage, as he was tired of riding; on which Lady Fanny muttered something, too, about 'a friend of grand-mamma's.'

'You should say a friend of yours, Fanny,' says Lady Jane: 'I am sure we should never have come to the Park if Fanny had not insisted upon bringing Mr. Titmarsh hither. Let me introduce the Earl of Tiptoff to Mr. Titmarsh.' But, instead of taking off his hat, as I did mine, his lordship growled out that he hoped for another opportunity, and galloped off again on his black horse. Why the deuce I should have offended him I never could understand.

But it semed as if I was destined to offend all the men that day; for who should presently come up but the Right Hon. Edmund Preston, one of his Majesty's Secretaries of State (as I knew very well by the almanac in our office) and the husband of Lady Jane.

The Right. Hon. Edmund was riding a grey cob, and was a fat pale-faced man, who looked as if he never went into the open air. 'Who the devil's that?' said he to his wife, looking surlily both at me and her.

'Oh, it's a friend of grandmamma's and Jane's,' said Lady Fanny at once, looking, like a sly rogue as she was, quite archly at her sister – who in her turn appeared quite fright-ened, and looked imploringly at her sister, and never dared to breathe a syllable. 'Yes, indeed,' continued Lady Fanny, 'Mr. Titmarsh is a cousin of grandmamma's by the mother's side: by the Hoggarty side. Didn't you know the Hoggarties when you were in Ireland, Edmund, with Lord Bagwig? Let me introduce you to grandmamma's cousin, Mr. Titmarsh; Mr. Titmarsh, my brother, Mr. Edmund Preston.'

There was Lady Jane all the time treading upon her sister's foot as hard as possible, and the little wicked thing would take no notice; and I, who had never heard of the cousinship, feeling as confounded as could be. But I did not know the Countess of Drum near so well as that sly minx her grand-daughter did; for the old lady, who had just before called poor Gus Hoskins her cousin, had, it appeared, the mania of fancying all the world related to her, and said, –

'Yes, we're cousins, and not very far removed. Mick Hoggarty's grandmother was Millicent Brady, and she and

my aunt Towzer were related, as all the world knows; for
Decimus Brady, of Ballybrady, married an own cousin of
aunt Towzer's mother, Bell Swift – that was no relation of the
Dean's, my love, who came but of a so-so family – and isn't
that clear?'

'Oh, perfectly, grandmamma,' said Lady Jane, laughing,
while the right honourable gent still rode by us, looking sour
and surly.

'And sure you knew the Hoggarties, Edmund? – the
thirteen redhaired girls – the nine graces, and four over, as
poor Clanboy used to call them. Poor Clan! – a cousin of
yours and mine, Mr. Titmarsh, and sadly in love with me he
was too. Not remember them *all* now, Edmund? – not
remember? – not remember Biddy and Minny, and Thedy
and Widdy, and Mysie and Grizzy, and Polly and Dolly, and
the rest?'

'D— the Miss Hoggarties, ma'am,' said the right honourable gent; and he said it with such energy, that his grey horse
gave a sudden lash out that well-nigh sent him over his head.
Lady Jane screamed; Lady Fanny laughed; old Lady Drum
looked as if she did not care twopence; and said, 'Serve you
right for swearing, you ojous man you!'

'Hadn't you better come into the carriage, Edmund – Mr.
Preston?' cried out the lady, anxiously.

'Oh, I'm sure I'll slip out, ma'am,' says I.

'Pooh – pooh! don't stir,' said Lady Drum: 'it's my carriage:
and if Mr. Preston chooses to swear at a lady of my years in
that ojous vulgar way – in that ojous vulgar way, I repeat – I
don't see why my friends should be inconvenienced for him.
Let him sit on the dicky if he likes, or come in and ride
bodkin.' It was quite clear that my Lady Drum hated her
grandson-in-law heartily; and I've remarked somehow in
families that this kind of hatred is by no means uncommon.

Mr. Preston, one of his Majesty's Secretaries of State, was,
to tell the truth, in a great fright upon his horse, and was glad
to get away from the kicking, plunging brute. His pale face
looked still paler than before, and his hands and legs trembled,
as he dismounted from the cob and gave the reins to his
servant. I disliked the looks of the chap – of the master, I mean
– at the first moment he came up, when he spoke rudely to

that nice gentle wife of his; and I thought he was a cowardly fellow, as the adventure of the cob showed him to be. Heaven bless you! a baby could have ridden it; and here was the man with his soul in his mouth at the very first kick.

'Oh, quick! *do* come in, Edmund,' said Lady Fanny, laughing; and the carriage steps being let down, and giving me a great scowl as he came in, he was going to place himself in Lady Fanny's corner (I warrant you I wouldn't budge from mine), when the little rogue cried out, 'Oh, no! by no means, Mr. Preston. Shut the door, Thomas. And oh! what fun it will be to show all the world a Secretary of State riding bodkin!'

And pretty glum the Secretary of State looked, I assure you!

'Take my place, Edmund, and don't mind Fanny's folly,' said Lady Jane, timidly.

'Oh, no! – pray, madam, don't stir! I'm comfortable, very comfortable; and so I hope is this Mr. – this gentleman.'

'Perfectly, I assure you,' says I. 'I was going to offer to ride your horse home for you, as you seemed to be rather frightened at it; but the fact was, I was so comfortable here that really I *couldn't* move.'

Such a grin as old Lady Drum gave when I said that! – how her little eyes twinkled, and her little sly mouth puckered up! I couldn't help speaking, for, look you, my blood was up.

'We shall always be happy of your company, cousin Titmarsh,' says she; and handed me a gold snuff-box, out of which I took a pinch, and sneezed with the air of a lord.

'As you have invited this gentleman into your carriage, Lady Jane Preston, hadn't you better invite him home to dinner?' says Mr. Preston quite blue with rage.

'I invited him into *my* carr'age,' says the old lady; 'and as we are going to dine at your house, and you press it, I'm sure I shall be very happy to see him there.'

'I'm very sorry I'm engaged,' said I.

'Oh, indeed, what a pity!' says Right Honourable Ned, still glowering at his wife. 'What a pity that this gentleman – I forget his name – that your friend, Lady Jane, is engaged! I am sure you would have had such gratification in meeting your relation in Whitehall.'

Lady Drum was over-fond of finding out relations to be sure; but this speech of Right Honourable Ned's was rather too much. 'Now, Sam,' says I, 'be a man and show your spirit!' So I spoke up at once, and said, 'Why, ladies, as the right honourable gent is so *very* pressing, I'll give up my engagement, and shall have sincere pleasure in cutting mutton with him. What's your hour, sir?'

He didn't condescend to answer, and for me I did not care; for, you see, I did not intend to dine with the man, but only to give him a lesson of manners. For though I am but a poor fellow, and hear people cry out how vulgar it is to eat pease with a knife, or ask three times for cheese, and such like points of ceremony, there's something, I think, much more vulgar than all this, and that is, insolence to one's inferiors. I hate the chap that uses it, as I scorn him of humble rank that affects to be of the fashion; and so I determined to let Mr. Preston know a piece of my mind.

When the carriage drove up to his house, I handed out the ladies as politely as possible, and walked into the hall, and then taking hold of Mr. Preston's button at the door, I said, before the ladies and the two big servants – upon my word I did – 'Sir,' says, I, 'this kind old lady asked me into her carriage, and I rode in it to please her, not myself. When you came up and asked who the devil I was, I thought you might have put the question in a more polite manner; but it wasn't my business to speak. When, by way of a joke, you invited me to dinner, I thought I would answer in a joke too, and here I am. But don't be frightened; I'm not a-going to dine with you: only if you play the same joke upon other parties – on some of the chaps in our office, for example – I recommend you to have a care, or they will *take you at your word.*'

'Is that all, sir?' says Mr. Preston, still in a rage: 'if you have done, will you leave this house, or shall my servants turn you out? Turn out this fellow! do you hear me?' and he broke away from me, and flung into his study in a rage.

'He's an ojous, horrid monsther of a man, that husband of yours!' said Lady Drum, seizing hold of her elder granddaughter's arm, 'and I hate him; and so come away, for the dinner'll be getting cold:' and she was for hurrying away Lady Jane without more ado. But that kind lady, coming forward, looking very pale and trembling, said, 'Mr. Titmarsh, I do hope you'll not be angry – that is, that you'll forget what has happened, for, believe me, it has given me very great – '

Very great what, I never could say, for here the poor thing's eyes filled with tears; and Lady Drum crying out 'Tut, tut! none of this nonsense,' pulled her away by the sleeve, and went upstairs. But little Lady Fanny walked boldly up to me, and held me out her little hand, and gave mine such a squeeze and said, 'Good-by, my dear Mr. Titmarsh,' so very kindly, that I'm blest if I did not blush up to the ears, and all the blood in my body began to tingle.

So, when she was gone, I clapped my hat on my head, and walked out of the hall-door, feeling as proud as a peacock and as brave as lion; and all I wished for was that one of those saucy, grinning footmen should say or do something to me that was the least uncivil, so that I might have the pleasure of knocking him down with my best compliments to his master. But neither of them did me any such favour! and I went away, and dined at home off boiled mutton and turnips with Gus Hoskins quite peacefully.

I did not think it was proper to tell Gus (who, between ourselves, is rather curious, and inclined to tittle-tattle,) all the particulars of the family quarrel of which I had been the cause and witness, and so just said that the old lady – ('They were the Drum arms,' says Gus, 'for I went and looked them out that minute in the "Peerage"') – that the old lady turned out to be a cousin of mine, and that she had taken me to drive in the Park. Next day we went to the office as usual, when you may be sure that Hoskins told everything of what had happened, and a great deal more; and somehow, though I did not pretend to care sixpence about the matter, I must confess that I *was* rather pleased that the gents in our office should hear of a part of my adventure.

But fancy my surprise, on coming home in the evening, to find Mrs. Stokes the landlady, Miss Selina Stokes her daughter, and Master Bob Stokes her son (an idle young vagabond that was always playing marbles on St. Bride's steps and in Salisbury Square), – when I found them all bustling and tumbling up the steps before me to our rooms

on the second floor, and there, on the table, between our two
flutes on one side, my album, Gus's 'Don Juan' and 'Peerage'
on the other, I saw as follows: –

1.   A basket of great red peaches, looking like the cheeks of
my dear Mary Smith.

2.   A ditto of large, fat, luscious, heavy-looking grapes.

3.   An enormous piece of raw mutton, as I thought it was;
but Mrs. Stokes said it was the primest haunch of venison that
ever she saw.

And three cards; viz.

DOWAGER COUNTESS OF DRUM.
LADY FANNY RAKES.

MR. PRESTON.
LADY JANE PRESTON.

EARL OF TIPTOFF.

'Sich a carriage!' says Mrs. Stokes (for that was the way the
poor thing spoke). 'Sich a carriage – all over coronites! sich
liveries – two great footmen, with red whiskers and yellow-
plush small-clothes; and inside, a very old lady in a white
poke-bonnet, and a young one with a great Leghorn hat and
blue ribands, and a great tall pale gentleman with a tuft on his
chin.

'"Pray, madam does Mr. Titmarsh live here?"' says the
young lady, with her clear voice.

'"Yes, my lady," says I; "but he's at the office – the West
Diddlesex Fire and Life Office, Cornhill."

'"Charles, get out the things," says the gentleman, quite
solemn.

'"Yes, my lord," says Charles; and brings me out the
haunch in a newspaper, and on the chany dish as you see it,
and the two baskets of fruit besides.

'"Have the kindness, madam," says my lord, "to take these
things to Mr. Titmarsh's rooms, with our, with Lady Jane
Preston's compliments, and request his acceptance of them;"
and then he pulled out the cards on your table, and this letter,
sealed with his lordship's own crown.'

And herewith Mrs. Stokes gave me a letter, which my wife keeps to this day, by the way, and which runs thus: –

'The Earl of Tiptoff has been commissioned by Lady Jane Preston to express her sincere regret and disappointment that she was not able yesterday to enjoy the pleasure of Mr. Titmarsh's company. Lady Jane is about to leave town immediately: she will therefore be unable to receive her friends in Whitehall Place this season. But Lord Tiptoff trusts that Mr. Titmarsh will have the kindness to accept some of the produce of her ladyship's garden and park; with which, perhaps, he will entertain some of those friends in whose favour he knows so well how to speak.'

Along with this was a little note containing the words 'Lady Drum at home. Friday evening, June 17.' And all this came to me because my aunt Hoggarty had given me a diamond-pin!

I did not send back the venison: as why should I? Gus was for sending it at once to Brough, our director; and the grapes and peaches to my aunt in Somersetshire.

'But no,' says I; 'we'll ask Bob Swinney and half-a-dozen more of our gents; and we'll have a merry night of it on Saturday.' And a merry night we had too; and as we had no wine in the cupboard, we had plenty of ale, and gin-punch afterwards. And Gus sat at the foot of the table, and I at the head; and we sang songs, both comic and sentimental, and drank toasts; and I made a speech that there is no possibility of mentioning here, because *entre nous*, I had quite forgotten in the morning everything that had taken place after a certain period on the night before.

CHAPTER IV

HOW THE HAPPY DIAMOND WEARER DINES AT PENTONVILLE

I Did not go to the office till half an hour after opening time on Monday. If the truth must be told, I was not sorry to let Hoskins have the start of me, and tell the chaps what had taken place, – for we all have little vanities, and I liked to be thought well of by my companions.

When I came in, I saw my business had been done, by the way in which the chaps looked at me; especially Abednego, who offered me a pinch out of his gold snuff-box the very first thing. Roundhand shook me, too, warmly by the hand, when he came round to look over my day-book, said I wrote a capital hand (and indeed I believe I do, without any sort of flattery), and invited me for dinner next Sunday, in Myddelton Square. 'You won't have,' said he, 'quite such a grand turn-out as with *your friends at the West End*' – he said this with a particular accent – 'but Amelia and I are always happy to see a friend in our plain way, – pale sherry, old port, and cut and come again. Hey?'

I said I would come, and bring Hoskins too.

He answered that I was very polite, and that he should be very happy to see Hoskins; and we went accordingly at the appointed day and hour; but though Gus was eleventh clerk and I twelfth, I remarked that at dinner I was helped first and best. I had twice as many forced-meat balls as Hoskins in my mock-turtle, and pretty nearly all the oysters out of the sauce-boat. Once, Roundhand was going to help Gus before me; when his wife, who was seated at the head of the table, looking very big and fierce in red crape and a turban, shouted out 'ANTONY!' and poor R. dropped the plate, and blushed as red as anything. How Mrs. R. did talk to me about the West End to be sure! She had a 'Peerage,' as you may be certain, and knew everything about the Drum family in a manner that

quite astonished me. She asked me how much Lord Drum had
a year; whether I thought he had twenty, thirty, forty, or a
hundred and fifty thousand a year; whether I was invited to
Drum Castle; what the young ladies wore, and if they had
those odious *gigot* sleeves which were just coming in then; and
here Mrs. R. looked at a pair of large mottled arms that she
was very proud of.

'I say, Sam my boy!' cried, in the midst of our talk, Mr.
Roundhand, who had been passing the port-wine round
pretty freely, 'I hope you looked to the main chance, and put
in a few shares of the West Diddlesex, – hey?'

'Mr. Roundhand, have you put up the decanters downstairs?' cries the lady, quite angry, and wishing to stop the
conversation.

'No, Milly, I've *emptied* 'em,' says R.

'Don't Milly me sir! and have the goodness to go down and
tell Lancy my maid' (*a look at me*) 'to make the tea in the study.
We have a gentleman here who is not *used* to Pentonville ways'
(*another look*); 'but he won't mind the ways of *friends*.' And here
Mrs. Roundhand heaved her very large chest, and gave me a
third look that was so severe, that I declare to goodness it made
me look quite foolish. As to Gus, she never so much as spoke to
him all the evening; but he consoled himself with a great lot of
muffins, and sat most of the evening (it was a cruel hot
summer) whistling and talking with Roundhand on the veran-
dah. I think I should like to have been with them, – for it was
very close in the room with that great big Mrs. Roundhand
squeezing close up to one on the sofa.

'Do you recollect what a jolly night we had here last
summer?' I heard Hoskins say, who was leaning over the
balcony, and ogling the girls coming home from church. 'You
and me with our coats off, plenty of cold rum-and- water, Mrs.
Roundhand at Margate, and a whole box of Manillas?'

'Hush!' said Roundhand, quite eagerly; 'Milly will hear.'

But Milly didn't hear: for she was occupied in telling me an
immense long story about her waltzing with the Count de
Schloppenzollern at the City ball to the Allied Sovereigns; and
how the count had great large white moustaches; and how
odd she thought it to go whirling round the room with a great
man's arm round your waist. 'Mr. Roundhand has never

allowed it since our marriage – never; but in the year 'fourteen
it was considered a proper compliment, you know, to pay the
sovereigns. So twenty-nine young ladies, of the best families
in the city of London, I assure you, Mr. Titmarsh – there was
the Lord Mayor's own daughters; Alderman Dobbin's gals:
Sir Charles Hopper's three, who have the great house in Baker
Street; and your humble servant, who was rather slimmer in
those days – twenty-nine of us had a dancing-master on
purpose, and practised waltzing in a room over the Egyptian
Hall at the Mansion House. He was a splendid man, that
Count Schloppenzollern!'

'I am sure, ma'am,' says I, 'he had a splendid partner!' and
blushed up to my eyes when I said it.

'Get away, you naughty creature!' says Mrs. Roundhand,
giving me a great slap: 'you're all the same, you men in the
West End – all deceivers. The count was just like you. Heigho!
Before you marry, it's all honey and compliments; when you
win us, it's all coldness and indifference. Look at Roundhand,
the great baby, trying to beat down a butterfly with his yellow
bandanna! Can a man like *that* comprehend me? can he fill the
void in my heart?' (She pronounced it without the *h*; but that
there should be no mistake, laid her hand upon the place
meant.) 'Ah, no! Will *you* be so neglectful when *you* marry,
Mr. Titmarsh?'

As she spoke, the bells were just tolling the people out of
church, and I fell a-thinking of my dear, dear Mary Smith in
the country, walking home to her grandmother's, in her
modest grey cloak, as the bells were chiming and the air full of
the sweet smell of the hay, and the river shining in the sun, all
crimson, purple, gold, and silver. There was my dear Mary a
hundred and twenty miles off, in Somersetshire, walking
home from church along with Mr. Snorter's family, with
which she came and went; and I was listening to the talk of
this great leering, vulgar woman.

I could not help feeling for a certain half of a sixpence that
you have heard me speak of; and putting my hand mechani-
cally upon my chest, I tore my fingers with the point of my
new DIAMOND-PIN. Mr. Polonius had sent it home the night
before, and I sported it for the first time at Roundhand's to
dinner.

'It's a beautiful diamond,' said Mrs. Roundhand. 'I have been looking at it all dinner-time. How rich you must be to wear such splendid things! and how can you remain in a vulgar office in the city – you who have such great acquaintances at the West End?'

The woman had somehow put me in such a passion that I bounced off the sofa, and made for the balcony without answering a word, – ay, and half broke my head against the sash, too, as I went out to the gents in the open air. 'Gus,' says I, 'I feel very unwell: I wish you'd come home with me.' And Gus did not desire anything better; for he had ogled the last girl out of the last church, and the night was beginning to fall.

'What! already?' said Mrs. Roundhand; 'there is a lobster coming, – a trifling refreshment; not what he's accustomed to, but – '

I am sorry to say I nearly said, 'D— the lobster!' as Roundhand went and whispered to her that I was ill.

'Ay,' said Gus, looking very knowing. 'Recollect, Mrs. R., that he was *at the West End* on Thursday, asked to dine, ma'am, with the tip-top nobs. Chaps don't dine at the West End for nothing, do they, R.? If you play at *bowls*, you know –'

'You must look out for *rubbers*,' said Roundhand, as quick as thought.

'Not in my house of a Sunday,' said Mrs. R., looking very fierce and angry. 'Not a card shall be touched *here*. Are we in a Protestant land, sir? in a Christian country?'

'My dear, you don't understand. We were not talking of rubbers of whist.'

'There shall be *no* game at all in the house of a Sabbath eve,' said Mrs. Roundhand; and out she flounced from the room, without ever so much as wishing us good-night.

'Do stay,' said the husband, looking very much frightened, – 'do stay. She won't come back while you're here; and I do wish you'd stay so.'

But we wouldn't: and when we reached Salisbury Square, I gave Gus a lecture about spending his Sundays idly; and read out one of Blair's sermons before we went to bed. As I turned over in bed, I could not help thinking about the luck the pin had brought me: and it was not over yet, as you will see in the next chapter.

CHAPTER V

HOW THE DIAMOND INTRODUCES HIM TO A STILL MORE FASHIONABLE PLACE

To tell the truth, though, about the pin, although I mentioned it almost the last thing in the previous chapter, I assure you it was by no means the last thing in my thoughts. I had come home from Mr. Polonius's, as I said, on Saturday night; and Gus and I happened to be out enjoying ourselves, half-price, at Sadler's Wells; and perhaps we took a little refreshment on our way back: but that has nothing to do with my story.

On the table, however, was the little box from the jeweller's; and when I took it out, – *my,* how the diamond did twinkle and glitter by the light of our one candle!

'I'm sure it would light up the room of itself,' says Gus. 'I've read they do in – in history.'

It was in the history of Cogia Hassan Alhabbal, in the 'Arabian Nights,' as I knew very well. But we put the candle out, nevertheless, to try.

'Well, I declare to goodness it does illuminate the old place!' says Gus; but the fact was, that there was a gas-lamp opposite our window, and I believe that was the reason why we could see pretty well. At least, in my bedroom, to which I was obliged to go without a candle, and of which the window looked out on a dead wall, I could not see a wink, in spite of the Hoggarty diamond, and was obliged to grope about in the dark for a pincushion which Somebody gave me (I don't mind owning it was Mary Smith), and in which I stuck it for the night. But, somehow, I did not sleep much for thinking of it, and woke very early in the morning; and, if the truth must be told, stuck it in my night-gown, like a fool, and admired myself very much in the glass.

Gus admired it as much as I did; for since my return, and especially since my venison dinner and drive with Lady

Drum, he thought I was the finest fellow in the world, and boasted about his 'West End friend' everywhere.

As we were going to dine at Roundhand's, and I had no black satin stock to set it off, I was obliged to place it in the frill of my best shirt, which tore the muslin sadly, by the way. However, the diamond had its effect on my entertainers, as we have seen; rather too much perhaps on one of them; and next day I wore it down at the office, as Gus would make me do; though it did not look near so well in the second day's shirt as on the first day, when the linen was quite clear and bright with Somersetshire washing.

The chaps at the West Diddlesex all admired it hugely, except that snarling Scotchman M'Whirter, fourth clerk – out of envy because I did not think much of a great yellow stone, named a carum-gorum, or some such thing, which he had in a snuff-mull, as he called it, – all except M'Whirter, I say, were delighted with it; and Abednego himself, who ought to know, as his father was in the line, told me the jewel was worth at least ten pounds, and that his governor would give me as much for it.

'That's a proof,' says Roundhand, 'that Tit's diamond is worth at least thirty.' And we all laughed, and agreed it was.

Now I must confess that all these praises, and the respect that was paid me, turned my head a little; and as all the chaps said I *must* have a black satin stock to set the stone off, I was fool enough to buy a stock that cost me five-and-twenty shillings, at Ludlam's in Piccadilly: for Gus said I must go to the best place, to be sure, and have none of our cheap and common East End stuff. I might have had one for sixteen and six in Cheapside, every whit as good; but when a young lad becomes vain, and wants to be fashionable, you see he can't help being extravagant.

Our director, Mr. Brough, did not fail to hear of the haunch of venison business, and my relationship with Lady Drum and the Right Hon. Edmund Preston: only Abednego, who told him, said I was her ladyship's first cousin; and this made Brough think more of me, and no worse than before.

Mr. B. was, as everybody knows, Member of Parliament for Rottenburgh; and being considered one of the richest men in the city of London, used to receive all the great people of the land at his villa at Fulham; and we often read in the papers of the rare doings going on there.

Well, the pin certainly worked wonders: for not content merely with making me a present of a ride in a countess's carriage, of a haunch of venison and two baskets of fruit, and the dinner at Roundhand's above described, my diamond had other honours in store for me, and procured me the honour of an invitation to the house of our director, Mr. Brough.

Once a year, in June, that honourable gent gave a grand ball at his house at Fulham; and by the accounts of the entertainment brought back by one or two of our chaps who had been invited, it was one of the most magnificent things to be seen about London. You saw Members of Parliment there as thick as peas in July, lords and ladies without end. There was everything and everybody of the tiptop sort; and I have heard that Mr. Gunter, of Berkeley Square, supplied the ices, supper, and footmen, – though of the latter Brough kept a plenty, but not enough to serve the host of people who came to him. The party, it must be remembered, was *Mrs.* Brough's party, not the gentleman's, – he being in the Dissenting way, would scarcely sanction any entertainments of the kind: but he told his City friends that his lady governed him in everything; and it was generally observed that most of them would allow their daughters to go to the ball if asked, on account of the immense number of the nobility which our director assembled together: Mrs. Roundhand, I know, for one, would have given one of her ears to go; but, as I have said before, nothing would induce Brough to ask her.

Roundhand himself, and Gutch, nineteenth clerk, son of the brother of an East Indian director, were the only two of our gents invited, as we knew very well: for they had received their invitations many weeks before, and bragged about them not a little. But two days before the ball, and after my diamond-pin had had its due effect upon the gents at the office, Abednego, who had been in the directors' room, came to my desk with a great smirk, and said, 'Tit, Mr. B. says that he expects you will come down with Roundhand to the ball on Thursday.' I thought Moses was joking, – at any rate, that Mr. B's messsage was a queer one; for people don't usually send invitations in that abrupt, peremptory sort of way; but sure enough, he presently came down himself and confirmed it, saying, as he was going out of the office, 'Mr. Titmarsh, you will come down on Thursday to Mrs. Brough's party, where you will see some relations of yours.'

'West End again!' says that Gus Hoskins; and accordingly down I went, taking a place in a cab which Roundhand hired for himself, Gutch, and me, and for which he very generously paid eight shillings.

There is no use to describe the grand gala, nor the number of lamps in the lodge and in the garden, nor the crowd of carriages that came in at the gates, nor the troops of curious people outside; nor the ices, fiddlers, wreaths of flowers, and cold supper within. The whole description was beautifully given in a fashionable paper, by a reporter who observed the same from the 'Yellow Lion' over the way, and told it in his journal in the most accurate manner; getting an account of the dresses of the great people from their footmen and coachmen when they came to the ale-house for their porter. As for the names of the guests, they, you may be sure, found their way to the same newspaper: and a great laugh was had at my expense, because among the titles of the great people mentioned my name appeared in the list of the 'Honourables.' Next day, Brough advertised 'a hundred and fifty guineas reward for an emerald necklace lost at the party of John Brough, Esq., at Fulham;' though some of our people said that no such thing was lost at all, and that Brough only wanted to advertise the magnificence of his society; but this doubt was raised by persons not invited, and envious no doubt.

Well, I wore my diamond, as you may imagine, and rigged myself in my best clothes, viz. my blue coat and brass buttons before mentioned, nankeen trousers and silk stockings, a white waistcoat, and a pair of white gloves bought for the occasion. But my coat was of country make, very high in the waist and short in the sleeves, and I suppose must have looked rather odd to some of the great people assembled, for they stared at me a great deal, and a whole crowd formed to see me dance – which I did to the best of my power, performing all the steps accurately and with great agility, as I had been taught by our dancing-master in the country.

And with whom do you think I had the honour to dance? With no less a person than Lady Jane Preston; who, it appears, had not gone out of town, and who shook me most kindly by the hand when she saw me, and asked me to dance with her. We had my Lord Tiptoff and Lady Fanny Rakes for our vis-à-vis.

You should have seen how the people crowded to look at us, and admired my dancing too, for I cut the very best of capers, quite different to the rest of the gents (my lord among the number), who walked through the quadrille as if they thought it a trouble, and stared at my activity with all their might. But when I have a dance I like to enjoy myself: and Mary Smith often said I was the very best partner at our assemblies. While we were dancing, I told Lady Jane how Roundhand, Gutch, and I, had come down three in a cab, besides the driver; and my account of our adventures made her ladyship laugh, I warrant you. Lucky it was for me that I didn't go back in the same vehicle; for the driver went and intoxicated himself at the 'Yellow Lion,' threw out Gutch and our head clerk as he was driving them back, and actually fought Gutch afterwards and blacked his eye, because he said that Gutch's red velvet waistcoat frightened the horse.

Lady Jane, however, spared me such an uncomfortable ride home: for she said she had a fourth place in her carriage, and asked me if I would accept it; and positively, at two o'clock in the morning, there was I, after setting the ladies and my lord down, driven to Salisbury Square in a great thundering carriage, with flaming lamps and two tall footmen, who nearly knocked the door and the whole little street down with the noise they made at the rapper. You should have seen Gus's head peeping out of the window in his white nightcap! He kept me up the whole night telling him about the ball, and the great people I had seen there; and next day he told at the office my stories, with his own usual embroideries upon them.

'Mr. Titmarsh,' said Lady Fanny, laughing to me, 'who is that great fat, curious man, the master of the house? Do you know he asked me if you were not related to us? and I said, "Oh, yes, you were."'

'Fanny!' says Lady Jane.

'Well,' answered the other, 'did not grandmamma say Mr. Titmarsh was her cousin?'

'But you know that grandmamma's memory is not very good.'

'Indeed, you're wrong, Lady Jane,' says my lord; 'I think it's prodigious.'

'Yes, but not very – not very accurate.'

'No, my lady,' says I; 'for her ladyship, the Countess of Drum, said, if you remember, that my friend Gus Hoskins – '

'Whose cause you supported so bravely,' cries Lady Fanny.

' – That my friend Gus is her ladyship's cousin too, which cannot be, for I know all his family: they live in Skinner Street and St. Mary Axe, and are not – not quite so *respectable* as *my* relatives.'

At this they all began to laugh; and my lord said, rather haughtily, –

'Depend upon it, Mr. Titmarsh, that Lady Drum is no more your cousin than she is the cousin of your friend Mr. Hoskinson.'

'Hoskins, my lord – and so I told Gus; but you see he is very fond of me, and *will* have it that I am related to Lady D.: and say what I will to the contrary, tells the story everywhere. Though to be sure,' added I, with a laugh, 'it has gained me no small good in my time.' So I described to the party our dinner at Mrs. Roundhand's, which all came from my diamond-pin, and my reputation as a connection of the aristocracy. Then I thanked Lady Jane handsomely for her magnificent present of fruit and venison, and told her that it had entertained a great number of kind friends of mine, who had drunk her ladyship's health with the greatest gratitude.

'*A haunch of venison!*' cried Lady Jane, quite astonished; 'indeed, Mr. Titmarsh, I am quite at a loss to understand you.'

As we passed a gas-lamp, I saw Lady Fanny laughing as usual, and turning her great arch sparkling black eyes at Lord Titptoff.

'Why, Lady Jane,' said he, 'if the truth must out, the great haunch of venison trick was one of this young lady's performing. You must know that I had received the above-named haunch from Lord Guttlebury's park; and knowing that Preston is not averse to Guttlebury venison, was telling Lady

Drum (in whose carriage I had a seat that day, as Mr. Titmarsh was not in the way) that I intended the haunch for your husband's table. Whereupon my Lady Fanny, clapping together her little hands, declared and vowed that the venison should *not* go to Preston, but should be sent to a gentleman about whose adventures on the day previous we had just been talking, – to Mr. Titmarsh, in fact; whom Preston, as Fanny vowed, had used most cruelly, and to whom, she said, a reparation was due. So my Lady Fanny insists upon our driving straight to my rooms in the 'Albany' (you know I am only to stay in my bachelor's quarters a month longer) – '

'Nonsense!' says Lady Fanny.

' – Insists upon driving straight to my chambers in the 'Albany,' extracting thence the above-named haunch – '

'Grandmamma was very sorry to part with it,' cries Lady Fanny.

' – And then she orders us to proceed to Mr. Titmarsh's house in the city, where the venison was left, in company with a couple of baskets of fruit bought at Grange's by Lady Fanny herself.'

'And what was more,' said Lady Fanny, 'I made grand-mamma go into Fr— into Lord Tiptoff's rooms, and dictated out of my own mouth the letter which he wrote, and pinned up the haunch of venison that his hideous old housekeeper brought us – I am quite jealous of her – I pinned up the haunch of venison in a copy of the *John Bull* newspaper.'

It had one of the Ramsbottom letters in it, I remember, which Gus and I read on Sunday at breakfast, and we nearly killed ourselves with laughing. The ladies laughed too when I told them this; and good-natured Lady Jane said she would forgive her sister, and hoped I would too: which I promised to do as often as her ladyship chose to repeat the offence.

I never had any more venison from the family; but I'll tell you *what* I had. About a month after came a card of 'Lord and Lady Tiptoff,' and a great piece of plum-cake; of which, I am sorry to say, Gus ate a great deal too much.

CHAPTER VI

OF THE WEST DIDDLESEX ASSOCIATION, AND OF THE EFFECT THE DIAMOND HAD THERE

Well, the magic of the pin was not over yet. Very soon after Mrs. Brough's grand party, our director called me up to his room at the West Diddlesex, and after examining my accounts, and speaking a while about business, said, 'That's a very fine diamond-pin, Master Titmarsh' (he spoke in a grave, patronizing way), 'and I called you on purpose to speak to you upon the subject. I do not object to seeing the young men of this establishment well and handsomely dressed; but I know that their salaries cannot afford ornaments like those, and I grieve to see you with a thing of such value. You have paid for it, sir – I trust you have paid for it; for, of all things, my dear – dear young friend, beware of debt.'

I could not conceive why Brough was reading me this lecture about debt and my having bought the diamond-pin, as I knew that he had been asking about it already, and how I came by it – Abednego told me so. 'Why, sir,' says I, 'Mr. Abednego told me that he had told you that I had told him – '

'Oh, ay – by-the-by, now I recollect, Mr. Titmarsh – I *do* recollect – yes; though I suppose, sir, you will imagine that I have other more important things to remember.'

'Oh, sir, in course,' says I.

'That one of the clerks *did* say something about a pin – that one of the other gentlemen had it. And so your pin was given you, was it?'

'It was given me, sir, by my aunt, Mrs. Hoggarty, of Castle Hoggarty,' said I, raising my voice; for I was a little proud of Castle Hoggarty.

'She must be very rich to make such presents, Titmarsh?'

'Why, thank you, sir,' says I, 'she *is* pretty well off. Four hundred a year jointure; a farm at Slopperton, sir; three houses

40

at Squashtail; and three thousand two hundred loose cash at the banker's, as I happen to know, sir – *that's all.*'

I did happen to know this, you see; because, while I was down in Somersetshire, Mr. MacManus, my aunt's agent in Ireland, wrote to say that a mortgage she had on Lord Brallaghan's property had just been paid off, and that the money was lodged at Coutts's. Ireland was in a very disturbed state in those days; and my aunt wisely determined not to invest her money in that country any more, but to look out for some good security in England. However, as she had always received six per cent. in Ireland, she would not hear of a smaller interest; and had warned me, as I was a commercial man, on coming to town, to look out for some means by which she could invest her money at that rate at least.

'And how do you come to know Mrs. Hoggarty's property so accurately?' said Mr. Brough; upon which I told him.

'Good heavens, sir! and do you mean that you, a clerk in the West Diddlesex Insurance Office, applied to by a respectable lady as to the manner in which she should invest property, never spoke to her about the Company which you have the honour to serve? Do you mean, sir, that you, knowing there was a bonus of five per cent. for yourself upon shares taken, did not press Mrs. Hoggarty to join us?'

'Sir,' says I, 'I'm an honest man, and would not take a bonus from my own relation.'

'Honest I know you are, my boy – give me your hand! So am I honest – so is every man in this Company honest; but we must be prudent as well. We have five millions of capital on our books, as you see – five *bonâ-fide* millions of *bonâ-fide* sovereigns paid up, sir, – there is no dishonesty there. But why should we not have twenty millions – a hundred millions? Why should not this be the greatest commercial association in the world! – as it shall be, sir – it shall, as sure as my name is John Brough, if heaven bless my honest endeavours to establish it! But do you suppose that it can be so, unless every man among us use his utmost exertions to forward the success of the enterprise? Never, sir, – never; and, for me, I say so everywhere. I glory in what I do. There is not a house in which I enter, but I leave a prospectus of the West Diddlesex. There is not a single tradesman I employ, but has shares in it to some amount. My servants, sir, – my very servants and grooms, are bound up with it. And the first question I ask of any one who applies to me for a place is, Are you insured or a shareholder in the West Diddlesex? the second, Have you a good character? And if the first question is answered in the negative, I say to the party coming to me, Then *be* a shareholder before you ask for a place in my household. Did you not see me – me, John Brough, whose name is good for millions – step out of my coach-and-four into this office, with four pounds nineteen, which I paid in to Mr. Roundhand as the price of half a share for the porter at my lodge-gate? Did you remark that I deducted a shilling from the five pound?'

'Yes, sir; it was the day you drew out eight hundred and seventy-three ten and six – Thursday week,' says I.

'And why did I deduct that shilling, sir? Because it was *my commission* – John Brough's commission of five per cent.; honestly earned by him, and openly taken. Was there any disguise about it? No. Did I do it for the love of a shilling? No,' says Brough, laying his hand on his heart, 'I did it from *principle* – from that motive which guides every one of my actions, as I can look up to heaven and say. I wish all my young men to see my example, and follow it: I wish – I pray that they may. Think of that example, sir. That porter of mine has a sick wife and nine young children: he is himself a sick man, and his tenure of life is feeble; he has earned money, sir, in my service – sixty pounds and more – it is all his children have to look to – all: but for that, in the event of his death, they would be houseless beggars in the street. And what have I done for that family, sir? I have put that money out of the reach of Robert Gates, and placed it so that it shall be a blessing to his family at his death. Every farthing is invested in shares in this office; and Robert Gates, my lodge-porter, is a holder of three shares in the West Diddlesex Association, and, in that capacity, your master and mine. Do you think I want to *cheat* Gates?'

'Oh, sir!' says I.

'To cheat that poor helpless man, and those tender, inno-cent children! – you can't think so, sir; I should be a disgrace to human nature if I did. But what boots all my energy and perseverance? What though I place my friends' money, my family's money, my own money – my hopes, wishes, desires, ambitions – all upon this enterprise? You young men will not do so. You, whom I treat with love and confidence as my children, make no return to *me*. When I toil, you remain still; when I struggle, you look on. Say the word at once, – you *doubt* me! O heavens, that *this* should be the reward of all my care and love for you!'

Here Mr. Brough was so affected that he actually burst into tears, and I confess I saw in its true light the negligence of which I had been guilty.

'Sir,' says I, 'I am very – very sorry: it was a matter of delicacy, rather than otherwise, which induced me not to speak to my aunt about the West Diddlesex.'

'Delicacy, my dear, dear boy – as if there can be any delicacy about making your aunt's fortune! Say indifference to me, say ingratitude, say folly, but don't say delicacy – no, no, not delicacy. Be honest, my boy, and call things by their right names – always do.'

'It *was* folly and ingratitude, Mr. Brough,' says I: 'I see it all now; and I'll write to my aunt this very post.'

'You had better do no such thing,' says Brough, bitterly: 'the stocks are at ninety, and Mrs. Hoggarty can get three per cent. for her money.'

'I *will* write, sir, – upon my word and honour, I will write.'

'Well, as your honour is passed, you must, I suppose; for never break your word – no, not in a trifle, Titmarsh. Send me up the letter when you have done, and I'll frank it – upon my word and honour I will,' says Mr. Brough, laughing, and holding out his hand to me.

I took it, and he pressed mine very kindly, – 'You may as well sit down here,' says he, as he kept hold of it; 'there is plenty of paper.'

And so I sat down and mended a beautiful pen, and began and wrote, 'Independent West Diddlesex Association, June, 1822,' and 'My dear Aunt,' in the best manner possible. Then I paused a little, thinking what I should next say; for I have always found that difficulty about letters. The date and my dear so-and-so one writes off immediately – it is the next part which is hard; and I put my pen in my mouth, flung myself back in my chair, and began to think about it.

'Bah!' said Brough, 'are you going to be about that letter all day, my good fellow? Listen to me, and I'll dictate to you in a moment.' So he began: –

'MY DEAR AUNT, – Since my return from Somersetshire, I am very happy indeed to tell you that I have so pleased the managing director of our Association and the Board, that they have been good enough to appoint me third clerk – '

'Sir!' says I.

'Write what I say. Mr Roundhand, as has been agreed by the board yesterday, quits the clerk's desk, and takes the title of secretary and actuary. Mr. Highmore takes his place; Mr. Abednego follows him; and I place you as third clerk – as

'third clerk (write), with a salary of a hundred and fifty pounds per annum. This news will, I know, gratify my dear mother and you, who have been a second mother to me all my life.

'When I was last at home, I remember you consulted me as to the best mode of laying out a sum of money which was lying useless in your bankers' hands. I have since lost no opportunity of gaining what information I could: and situated here as I am, in the very midst of affairs, I believe, although very young, I am as good a person to apply to as many others of greater age and standing.

'I frequently thought of mentioning to you our Association, but feelings of delicacy prevented me from doing so. I did not wish that any one should suppose that a shadow of self-interest could move me in any way.

'But I believe, without any sort of doubt, that the West Diddlesex Association offers the best security that you can expect for your capital, and, at the same time, the highest interest you can anywhere procure.

'The situation of the Company, as I have it from *the very best authority* (underline that), is as follows:-

'The subscribed and *bonâ-fide* capital is FIVE MILLIONS STERLING.

'The body of directors you know. Suffice it to say that the managing director is John Brough, Esq., of the firm of Brough and Hoff, a Member of Parliament, and a man as well known as Mr. Rothschild in the city of London. His private fortune, I know for a fact, amounts to half a million; and the last dividends paid to the shareholders of the I. W. D. Association amounted to 6 per cent. per annum.'

[That I know was the dividend declared by us].

'Although the shares in the market are at a very great premium, it is the privilege of the four first clerks to dispose of a certain number, 5,000l. each at par; and if you, my dearest aunt, would wish for 2,500l. worth, I hope you will allow me to oblige you by offering you so much of my new privileges.

'Let me hear from you immediately upon the subject, as I have already an offer for the whole amount of my shares at market price.'

'But I haven't sir,' says I.

'You have, sir. I will take the shares; but I want you. I want as many respectable persons in the company as I can bring. I want you because I like you, and I don't mind telling you that I have views of my own as well; for I am an honest man and say openly what I mean, and I'll tell you why I want you. I can't, by the regulations of the company, have more than a certain number of votes, but if your aunt takes shares, I expect – I don't mind owning it – that she will vote with me. Now do you understand me? My object is to be all in all with the company; and if I be, I will make it the most glorious enterprise that ever was conducted in the city of London.'

So I signed the letter and left it with Mr. B. to frank.

The next day I went and took my place at the third clerk's desk, being led to it by Mr. B., who made a speech to the gents, much to the annoyance of the other chaps, who grumbled about their services: though, as for the matter of that, our services were very much alike: the company was only three years old, and the oldest clerk in it had not six months' more standing in it than I. 'Look out,' said that envious M'Whirter to me. 'Have you got money, or have any of your relations money? or are any of them going to put it into the concern?'

I did not think fit to answer him, but took a pinch out of his mull, and was always kind to him; and he, to say the truth, was always most civil to me. As for Gus Hoskins, he began to think I was a superior being; and I must say that the rest of the chaps behaved very kindly in the matter, and said that if one man were to be put over their heads before another, they would have pitched upon me, for I had never harmed any of them, and done little kindnesses to several.

'I know,' says Abednego, 'how you got the place. It was I who got it you. I told Brough you were a cousin of Preston's, the Lord of the Treasury, had venison from him, and all that; and depend upon it he expects that you will be able to do him some good in that quarter.'

I think there was some likelihood in what Abednego said, because our governor, as we called him, frequently spoke to me about my cousin; told me to push the concern in the West End of the town, get as many noblemen as we could to insure with us, and so on. It was in vain I said that I could do nothing with Mr. Preston. 'Bah! bah!' says Mr. Brough, 'don't tell *me*. People don't send haunches of venison to you for nothing;' and I'm convinced he thought I was a very cautious, prudent fellow, for not bragging about my great family, and keeping my connection with them a secret. To be sure he might have learned the truth from Gus, who lived with me; but Gus would insist that I was hand in glove with all the nobility, and boasted about me ten times as much as I did myself.

The chaps used to call me the 'West Ender.'

'See,' thought I, 'what I have gained by aunt Hoggarty giving me a diamond-pin! What a lucky thing it is that she did not give me the money, as I hoped she would! Had I not had the pin – had I even taken it to any other person but Mr. Polonius, Lady Drum would never have noticed me; had Lady Drum never noticed me, Mr. Brough never would, and I never should have been third clerk of the West Diddlesex.'

I took heart at all this, and wrote off on the very evening of my appointment to my dearest Mary Smith, giving her warning that a 'certain event,' for which one of us was longing very earnestly, might come off sooner than we had expected. And why not? Miss S.'s own fortune was 70*l.* a year, mine was 150*l.*, and when we had 300*l.*, we always vowed we would marry. 'Ah!' thought I, 'if I could but go to Somersetshire now, I might boldly walk up to old Smith's door' (he was her grandfather, and a half-pay lieutenant of the navy), 'I might knock at the knocker and see my beloved Mary in the parlour, and not be obliged to sneak behind hayricks on the look-out for her, or pelt stones at midnight at her window.'

My aunt, in a few days, wrote a pretty gracious reply to my letter. She had not determined, she said, as to the manner in which she should employ her three thousand pounds, but should take my offer into consideration; begging me to keep my shares open for a little while, until her mind was made up.

What, then, does Mr. Brough do? I learned afterwards, in the year 1830, when he and the West Diddlesex Association had disappeared altogether, how he had proceeded.

'Who are the attorneys at Slopperton?' says he to me in a careless way.

'Mr. Ruck, sir,' says I, 'is the Tory solicitor, and Messrs. Hodge and Smithers the Liberals.' I knew them very well, for the fact is, before Mary Smith came to live in our parts, I was rather partial to Miss Hodge, and her great gold-coloured ringlets; but Mary came and soon put *her* nose out of joint as the saying is.

'And you are of what politics?'

'Why, sir, we are Liberals.' I was rather ashamed of this, for Mr. Brough was an out-and-out Tory; but Hodge and Smithers is a most respectable firm. I brought up a packet from them to Hickson, Dixon, Paxton and Jackson, *our* solicitors, who are their London correspondents.

Mr. Brough only said. 'Oh, indeed!' and did not talk any further on the subject, but began admiring my diamond-pin very much.

'Titmarsh, my dear boy,' says he, 'I have a young lady at Fulham who is worth seeing, I assure you, and who has heard so much about you from her father (for I like you, my boy, I don't care to own it) that she is rather anxious to see you too. Suppose you come down to us for a week? Abednego will do your work.'

'Law sir! you are very kind,' says I.

'Well, you shall come down; and I hope you will like my claret. But hark ye! I don't think, my dear fellow, you are quite smart enough – quite well enough dressed. Do you understand me?'

'I've my blue coat and brass buttons at home, sir.'

'What! that thing with the waist between your shoulders that you wore at Mrs. Brough's party?' (It *was* rather high-waisted, being made in the country two years before.) 'No – no, that will never do. Get some new clothes, sir, – two new suits of clothes.'

'Sir!' says I, 'I'm already, if the truth must be told, very short of money for this quarter, and can't afford myself a new suit for a long time to come.'

'Pooh, pooh! don't let that annoy you. Here's a ten-pound note – but no, on second thoughts, you may as well go to my tailor's. I'll drive you down there: and never mind the bill, my good lad!' And drive me down he actually did, in his grand coach-and-four, to Mr. Von Stiltz, in Clifford Street, who took my measure, and sent me home two of the finest coats ever seen, a dress-coat and a frock, a velvet waistcoat, a silk ditto, and three pairs of pantaloons, of the most beautiful make. Brough told me to get some boots and pumps, and silk stockings for evenings; so that when the time came for me to go down to Fulham, I appeared as handsome as any young noble man, and Gus said that I looked, by jingo, like a regular tip-top swell.

In the meantime the following letter had been sent down to Hodge and Smithers: –

'DEAR SIRS, –
                    'Ram Alley, Cornhill, London,
                    July, 1822.

This part being on private affairs
relative to the cases of
Dixon *v*. Haggerstony,
Snodgrass *v*. Rubbidge and another,
I am not permitted
to extract.

'Likewise we beg to hand you a few more prospectuses of the Independent West Diddlesex Fire and Life Assurance Company, of which we have the honour to be the solicitors in London. We wrote to you last year, requesting you to accept the Slopperton and Somerset agency for the same, and have been expecting for some time back that either shares or assurances should be effected by you.

'The capital of the Company, as you know, is five millions sterling (say 5,000,000*l.*), and we are in a situation to offer more than the usual commission to our agents of the legal profession. We shall be happy to give a premium of 6 per cent. for shares to the amount of 1,000*l.*, 6½ per cent. above a thousand, to be paid immediately upon the taking of the shares.

I am, dear Sirs, for self and partners,

'Yours most faithfully,

'SAMUEL JACKSON.'

This letter, as I have said, came into my hands some time afterwards. I knew nothing of it in the year 1822, when, in my new suit of clothes, I went down to pass a week at the Rookery, Fulham residence of John Brough, Esq., M.P.

CHAPTER VII

HOW SAMUEL TITMARSH REACHED THE HIGHEST POINT OF PROSPERITY

If I had the pen of a George Robins, I might describe the Rookery properly: suffice it, however, to say, it is a very handsome country place; with handsome lawns sloping down to the river, handsome shrubberies and conservatories, fine stables, out-houses, kitchen-gardens, and everything belonging to a first-rate *rus in urbe*, as the great auctioneer called it when he hammered it down some years after.

I arrived on a Saturday at half an hour before dinner: a grave gentleman out of livery showed me to my room; a man in a chocolate coat and gold lace, with Brough's crest on the buttons, brought me a silver shaving-pot of hot water on a silver tray; and a grand dinner was ready at six, at which I had the honour of appearing in Von Stiltz's dress-coat and my new silk stockings and pumps.

Brough took me by the hand as I came in, and presented me to his lady, a stout, fair-haired woman, in light blue satin; then to his daughter, a tall, thin, dark-eyed girl with beetle-brows, looking very ill-natured, and about eighteen.

'Belinda my love,' said her papa, 'this young gentleman is one of my clerks, who was at our ball.'

'Oh, indeed!' says Belinda, tossing up her head.

'But not a common clerk, Miss Belinda, – so, if you please, we will have none of your aristocratic airs with him. He is a nephew of the Countess of Drum; and I hope he will soon be very high in our establishment, and in the city of London.'

At the name of Countess (I had a dozen times rectified the error about our relationship), Miss Belinda made a low courtesy, and stared at me very hard, and said she would try and make the Rookery pleasant to any friend of papa's. 'We have not much *monde* today,' continued Miss Brough, 'and are only in *petit comité*; but I hope before you leave us you will see some *société* that will make your *séjour* agreeable.'

I saw at once that she was a fashionable girl, from her using the French language in this way.

'Isn't she a fine girl?' said Brough, whispering to me, and evidently as proud of her as a man could be. 'Isn't she a fine girl – eh, you dog? Do you see breeding like that in Somerset-shire?'

'No, sir, upon my word!' answered I, rather slyly; for I was thinking all the while how 'Somebody' was a thousand times more beautiful, simple, and lady-like.

'And what has my dearest love been doing all day?' said her papa.

'Oh, Pa! I have *pincé*'d the harp a little to Captain Fizgig's flute. Didn't I, Captain Fizgig?'

Captain the Hon. Francis Fizgig said, 'Yes, Brough, your fair daughter *pincé*'d the harp, and *touché*'d the piano, and *égratigné*'d the guitar, and *écorché*'d a song or two; and we had the pleasure of a *promenade à l'eau*, – of a walk upon the water.'

'Law, captain!' cries Mrs. Brough, 'walk on the water?'

'Hush, mamma, you don't understand French!' says Miss Belinda, with a sneer.

'It's a sad disadvantage, madam,' says Fizgig, gravely; 'and I recommend you and Brough here, who are coming out in the great world, to have some lessons; or at least get up a couple of dozen phrases, and introduce them into your conversation here and there. I suppose, sir, you speak it commonly at the office, or what you call it?' And Mr. Fizgig put his glass into his eye and looked at me.

'We speak English, sir,' says I, 'knowing it better than French.'

'Everybody has not had your opportunities, Miss Brough,' continued the gentleman. 'Everybody has not *voyagé* like *nous autres*, hey? *Mais que voulez-vous*, my good sir? you must stick to your cursed ledgers and things. What's the French for ledger, Miss Belinda?'

'How can you ask! *Je n'en sais rien*, I'm sure.'

'You should learn, Miss Brough,' said her father. 'The daughter of a British merchant need not be ashamed of the means by which her father gets his bread. *I'm* not ashamed –

I'm not proud. Those who know John Brough, know that ten years ago he was a poor clerk like my friend Titmarsh here, and is now worth half a million. Is there any man in the House better listened to than John Brough? Is there any duke in the land that can give a better dinner than John Brough; or a larger fortune to his daughter than John Brough? Why, sir, the humble person now speaking to you could buy out many a German duke! But I'm not proud – no, no, not proud. There's my daughter – look at her – when I die she will be mistress of my fortune; but am I proud? No! Let him who can win her marry her, that's what I say. Be it you, Mr. Fizgig, son of a peer of the realm; or you, Bill Tidd. Be it a duke or a shoeblack, what do I care, hey? – what do I care?'

'O-o-oh!' signed the gent who went by the name of Bill Tidd: a very pale young man, with a black riband round his neck instead of a handkerchief, and his collars turned down like Lord Byron. He was leaning against the mantelpiece, and with a pair of great green eyes ogling Miss Brough with all his might.

'Oh, John – my dear John!' cried Mrs. Brough, seizing her husband's hand and kissing it, 'you are an angel, that you are!'

'Isabella, don't flatter me; I'm a *man*, – a plain, downright citizen of London, without a particle of pride, except in you and my daughter here – my two Bells, as I call them! This is the way that we live, Titmarsh my boy: ours is a happy, humble, Christian home, and that's all. Isabella, leave go my hand!'

'Mamma, you mustn't do so before company; it's odious!' shrieked Miss B.; and mamma quietly let the hand fall, and heaved from her ample bosom a great large sigh. I felt a liking for that simple woman, and a respect for Brough too, He *couldn't* be a bad man, whose wife loved him so.

Dinner was soon announced, and I had the honour of leading in Miss B., who looked back rather angrily, I thought, at Captain Fizgig, because that gentleman had offered his arm to Mrs. Brough. He sat on the right of Mrs. Brough, and Miss flounced down on the seat next to him, leaving me and Mr. Tidd to take our places at the opposite side of the table.

At dinner there was turbot and soup first, and boiled turkey afterwards of course. How is it that at all the great dinners they have this perpetual boiled turkey? It was real turtle-soup: the first time I had ever tasted it; and I remarked how Mrs. B., who insisted on helping it, gave all the green lumps of fat to her husband, and put several slices of the breast of the bird under the body, until it came to his turn to be helped.

'I'm a plain man,' says John, 'and eat a plain dinner. I hate your kickshaws, though I keep a French cook for those who are not of my way of thinking. I'm no egotist, look you; I've no prejudices; and Miss there has her bechamels and fallals according to her taste. Captain, try the *volly vong*.'

We had plenty of champagne and old madeira with dinner, and great silver tankards of porter, which those might take who chose. Brough made especially a boast of drinking beer: and, when the ladies retired, said, 'Gentlemen, Tiggins will give you an unlimited supply of wine: there's no stinting here;' and then laid himself down in his easy chair and fell asleep.

'He always does so,' whispered Mr. Tidd to me.

'Get some of that yellow-sealed wine, Tiggins,' says the captain. 'That other claret we had yesterday is loaded, and disagrees with me infernally!'

I must say I liked the yellow seal much better than aunt Hoggarty's Rosolio.

I soon found out what Mr. Tidd was, and what he was longing for.

'Isn't she a glorious creature?' says he to me.

'Who, sir?' says I.

'Miss Belinda, to be sure!' cried Tidd. 'Did mortal ever look upon eyes like hers, or view a more sylph-like figure?'

'She might have a little more flesh, Mr. Tidd,' says the captain, 'and a little less eyebrow. They look vicious, those scowling eyebrows, in a girl. *Qu'en dites-vous*, Mr. Titmarsh, as Miss Brough would say?'

'I think it remarkably good claret, sir,' says I.

'Egad, you're the right sort of fellow.' says the captain. '*Volto chiuso*, eh? You respect our sleeping host yonder?'

'That I do, sir, as the first man in the city of London, and my managing director.'

'And so do I,' says Tidd; 'and this day fortnight, when I'm of age, I'll prove my confidence too.'

'As how?' says I.

'Why, sir, you must know that I come into – ahem – a considerable property, sir, on the 14th of July, which my father made – in business.'

'Say at once he was a tailor, Tidd.'

'He *was* a tailor, sir, – but what of that? I've had a university education, and have the feelings of a gentleman; as much – ay, perhaps, and more, than some members of an effete aristocracy.'

'Tidd, don't be severe!' says the captain, drinking a tenth glass.

'Well, Mr. Titmarsh, when of age I come into a considerable property; and Mr. Brough has been so good as to say he can get me twelve hundred a year for my twenty thousand pounds, and I have promised to invest them.'

'In the West Diddlesex, sir?' says I – 'in our office?'

'No, in another company, of which Mr. Brough is director, and quite as good a thing. Mr. Brough is a very old friend of my family, sir, and he has taken a great liking to me; and he says that with my talents I ought to get into Parliament; and then – and then! after I have laid out my patrimony, I may look to *matrimony*, you see!'

'Oh, you designing dog!' said the captain. 'When I used to lick you at school, who ever would have thought that I was thrashing a sucking statesman?'

'Talk away, boys!' said Brough, waking out of his sleep: 'I only sleep with half an eye, and hear you all. Yes, you shall get into Parliament, Tidd my man, or my name's not Brough! You shall have six per cent. for your money, or never believe me! But as for my daughter – ask *her*, and not me. You, or the captain, or Titmarsh, may have her, if you can get her. All I ask in a son-in-law is, that he should be, as every one of you is, an honourable and highminded man!'

Tidd at this looked very knowing; and as our host sank off to sleep again, pointed archly at his eyebrows, and wagged his head at the captain.

'Bah!' says the captain. 'I say what I think; and you may tell Miss Brough if you like.' And so presently this conversation ended, and we were summoned in to coffee. After which the captain sang songs with Miss Brough; Tidd looked at her and said nothing; I looked at prints, and Mrs. Brough sat knitting stockings for the poor. The captain was sneering openly at Miss Brough and her affected ways and talk: but in spite of his bullying contemptuous way, I thought she seemed to have a great regard for him, and to bear his scorn very meekly.

At twelve Captain Fizgig went off to his barracks at Knightsbridge, and Tidd and I to our rooms. Next day being Sunday, a great bell woke us at eight, and at nine we all assembled in the breakfast-room, where Mr. Brough read prayers, a chapter, and made an exhortation afterwards, to us and all the members of the household; except the French cook, Monsieur Nongtongpaw, whom I could see, from my chair, walking about in the shrubberies in his white night-cap, smoking a cigar.

Every morning on week-days, punctually at eight, Mr. Brough went through the same ceremony, and had his family to prayers; but though this man was a hypocrite, as I found afterwards, I'm not going to laugh at the family prayers, or say he was a hypocrite *because* he had them. There are many bad and good men who don't go through the ceremony at all; but I am sure the good men would be the better for it, and am not called upon to settle the question with respect to the bad ones; and therefore I have passed over a great deal of the religious part of Mr. Brough's behaviour: suffice it, that religion was always on his lips; that he went to church thrice every Sunday, when he had not a party; and if he did not talk religion with us when we were alone, had a great deal to say upon the subject upon occasions, as I found one day when we had a Quaker and Dissenter party to dine, and when his talk was as grave as that of any minister present. Tidd was not there that day, – for nothing could make him forsake his Byron riband or refrain from wearing his collars turned down; so Tidd was sent with the buggy to Astley's. 'And hark ye, Titmarsh my boy,' said he, 'leave your diamond-pin upstairs: our friends to-day don't like such gew-gaws; and though for my part I am no enemy to harmless ornaments, yet I would not shock the feelings of those who have sterner opinions. You will see that my wife and Miss Brough consult my wishes in this respect.' And so they did, – for they both came down to dinner in black gowns and tippets; whereas Miss B. had commonly her dress half off her shoulders.

The captain rode over several times to see us; and Miss Brough seemed always delighted to see *him*. One day I met him as I was walking out alone by the river, and we had a long talk together.

'Mr. Titmarsh,' says he, 'from what little I have seen of you, you seem to be an honest straight-minded young fellow; and I want some information that you can give. Tell me, in the first place, if you will – and upon my honour it shall go no farther – about this Insurance Company of yours? You are in the city, and see how affairs are going on. Is your concern a stable one?'

'Sir,' said I, 'frankly then, and upon my honour too, I believe it is. It has been set up only four years, it is true; but Mr. Brough had a great name when it was established, and a vast connection. Every clerk in the office has, to be sure, in a manner, paid for his place, either by taking shares himself, or by his relations taking them. I got mine because my mother, who is very poor, devoted a small sum of money that came to us to the purchase of an annuity for herself and a provision for me. The matter was debated by the family and our attorneys, Messrs. Hodge and Smithers, who are very well known in our part of the country; and it was agreed on all hands that my mother could not do better with her money for all of us than invest it in this way. Brough alone is worth half a million of money, and his name is a host in itself. Nay, more: I wrote the other day to an aunt of mine, who has a considerable sum of money in loose cash, and who had consulted me as to the disposal of it, to invest it in our office. Can I give you any better proof of my opinion of its solvency?'

'Did Brough persuade you in any way?'

'Yes, he certainly spoke to me; but he very honestly told me his motives, and tells them to us all as honestly. He says, "Gentlemen, it is my object to increase the connection of the office as much as possible. I want to crush all the other offices in London. Our terms are lower than any office, and we can bear to have them lower, and a great business will come to us that way. But we must work ourselves as well. Every single shareholder and officer of the establishment must exert himself, and bring us customers, – no matter for how little they are engaged – engage them: that is the great point." And accordingly our director makes all his friends and servants shareholders: his very lodge-porter yonder is a shareholder; and he thus endeavours to fasten upon all whom he comes near. I, for instance, have just been appointed over the heads of our gents, to a much better place than I held. I am asked down here, and entertained royally; and why? Because my aunt has three thousand pounds which Mr. Brough wants her to invest with us.'

'That looks awkward, Mr. Titmarsh.'

'Not a whit, sir: he makes no disguise of the matter. When the question is settled one way or the other, I don't believe Mr. Brough will take any further notice of me. But he wants me now. This place happened to fall in just at the very moment when he had need of me; and he hopes to gain over my family through me. He told me as much as we drove down. "You are a man of the world, Titmarsh," said he; "you know that I don't give you this place because you are an honest fellow, and write a good hand. If I had had a lesser bribe to offer you at the moment, I should only have given you that; but I had no choice and gave you what was in my power."'

'That's fair enough; but what can make Brough so eager for such a small sum as three thousand pounds?'

'If it had been ten, sir, he would have been not a bit more eager. You don't know the city of London, and the passion which our great men in the share-market have for increasing their connection. Mr. Brough, sir, would canvass and wheedle a chimney-sweep in the way of business. See, here is poor Tidd and his twenty thousand pounds. Our director has taken possession of him just in the same way. He wants all the capital he can lay his hands on.'

'Yes, and suppose he runs off with the capital?'

'Mr. Brough, of the firm of Brough and Hoff, sir? Suppose the Bank of England runs off! But here we are at the lodge-gate. Let's ask Gates, another of Mr. Brough's victims.' And we went in and spoke to old Gates.

'Well, Mr. Gates,' says I, beginning the matter cleverly, 'you are one of my masters, you know, at the West Diddlesex yonder?'

'Yees, sure,' says old Gates, grinning. He was a retired servant, with a large family come to him in his old age.

'May I ask you what your wages are, Mr. Gates, that you can lay by so much money, and purchase shares in our company?'

Gates told us his wages; and when we inquired whether they were paid regularly, swore that his master was the kindest gentleman in the world; that he had put two of his daughters into service, two of his sons to charity-schools, made one apprentice, and narrated a hundred other benefits that he had received from the family. Mrs. Brough clothed half the children; master gave them blankets and coats in winter, and soup and meat all the year round. There never was such a generous family, sure, since the world began.

'Well, sir,' said I to the captain, 'does that satisfy you? Mr. Brough gives to these people fifty times as much as he gains from them; and yet he makes Mr. Gates take shares in our company.'

'Mr. Titmarsh,' says the captain, 'you are an honest fellow; and I confess your argument sounds well. Now tell me, do you know anything about Miss Brough and her fortune?'

'Brough will leave her everything – or says so.' But I suppose the captain saw some particular expression in my countenance, for he laughed and said, –

'I suppose, my dear fellow, you think she's dear at the price. Well, I don't know that you are far wrong.'

'Why then, if I may make so bold, Captain Fizgig, are you always at her heels?'

'Mr. Titmarsh,' says the captain, 'I owe twenty thousand pounds;' and he went back to the house directly, and proposed for her.

I thought this rather cruel and unprincipled conduct on the gentleman's part; for he had been introduced to the family by Mr. Tidd, with whom he had been at school, and had supplanted Tidd entirely in the great heiress's affections. Brough stormed, and actually swore at his daughter (as the captain told me afterwards,) when he heard that the latter had accepted Mr. Fizgig; and at last, seeing the captain, made him give his word that the engagement should be kept secret for a few months. And Captain F. only made a confidant of me, and the mess, as he said: but this was after Tidd had paid his twenty thousand pounds over to our governor, which he did punctually when he came of age. The same day, too, he proposed for the young lady, and I need not say was rejected. Presently the captain's engagement began to be whispered about: all his great relations, the Duke of Doncaster, the Earl of Cinqbars, the Earl of Crabs, &c., came and visited the Brough family; the Hon. Henry Ringwood became a shareholder in our company, and the Earl of Crabs offered to be. Our shares rose to a premium; our director, his lady, and daughter were presented at court; and the great West Diddlesex Association bid fair to be the first assurance office in the kingdom.

A very short time after my visit to Fulham, my dear aunt wrote to me to say that she had consulted with her attorneys, Messrs. Hodge and Smithers, who strongly recommended that she should invest the sum as I advised. She had the sum invested, too, in my name, paying me many compliments upon my honesty and talent; of which, she said, Mr. Brough had given her the most flattering account. And at the same time my aunt informed me that at her death the shares should be my own. This gave me a great weight in the company, as you may imagine. At our next annual meeting, I attended in my capacity as a shareholder, and had great pleasure in hearing Mr. Brough, in a magnificent speech, declare a dividend of six per cent, that we all received over the counter.

'You lucky young scoundrel!' said Brough to me: 'do you know what made me give you your place?'

'Why, my aunt's money, to be sure, sir,' said I.

'No such thing. Do you fancy I cared for those paltry three thousand pounds? I was told you were nephew of Lady Drum; and Lady Drum is grandmother of Lady Jane Preston; and Mr. Preston is a man who can do us a world of good. I knew that they had sent you venison, and the deuce knows what; and when I saw Lady Jane at my party shake you by the hand, and speak to you so kindly, I took all Abednego's tales for gospel. *That* was the reason you got the place, mark you, and not on account of your miserable three thousand pounds. Well, sir, a fortnight after you was with us at Fulham, I met Preston in the House, and made a merit of having given the place to his cousin. "Confound the insolent scoundrel!" said he; "*he* my cousin! I suppose you take all old Drum's stories for true? Why, man, it's her mania: she never is introduced to a man but she finds out a cousinship, and would not fail of course with that cur of a Titmarsh!" "Well," said I, laughing, "that cur has got a good place in consequence, and the matter can't be mended." So you see,' continued our director, 'that you were indebted for your place, not to your aunt's money, but – '

'But to MY AUNT'S DIAMOND-PIN!'

'Lucky rascal!' said Brough, poking me in the side and going out of the way. And lucky, in faith, I thought I was.

CHAPTER VIII

RELATES THE HAPPIEST DAY OF SAMUEL TITMARSH'S LIFE

I don't know how it was that in the course of the next six months Mr. Roundhand, the actuary, who had been such a profound admirer of Mr. Brough and the West Diddlesex Association, suddenly quarrelled with both, and taking his money out of the concern, he disposed of his 5,000*l*. worth of shares to a pretty good profit, and went away, speaking everything that was evil both of the company and the director.

Mr. Highmore now became secretary and actuary, Mr. Abednego was first clerk, and your humble servant was second in the office at a salary of 200*l*. a year. How unfounded were Mr. Roundhand's aspersions of the West Diddlesex appeared quite clearly at our meeting in January, 1823, when our chief director, in one of the most brilliant speeches ever heard, declared that the half-yearly dividend was 4*l*. per cent., at the rate of 8*l*. per cent., per annum; and I sent to my aunt 120*l*. sterling as the amount of the interest of the stock in my name.

My excellent aunt, Mrs. Hoggarty, delighted beyond measure, sent me back 10*l*. for my own pocket, and asked me if she had not better sell Slopperton and Squashtail, and invest all her money in this admirable concern.

On this point I could not surely do better than ask the opinion of Mr. Brough. Mr. B. told me that shares could not be had but at a premium; but on my representing that I knew of 5,000*l*. worth in the market at par, he said, – 'Well, if so, he would like a fair price for his, and would not mind disposing of 5,000*l*. worth, as he had rather a glut of West Diddlesex shares, and his other concerns wanted feeding with ready money.' At the end of our conversation, of which I promised

61

to report the purport to Mrs. Hoggarty, the director was so kind as to say that he had determined on creating a place of private secretary to the managing director, and that I should hold that office with an additional salary of 150*l.*

I had 250*l.* a year, Miss Smith had 70*l.* per annum to her fortune. What had I said should be my line of conduct whenever I could realize 300*l.* a year?

Gus of course, and all the gents in our office through him, knew of my engagement with Mary Smith. Her father had been a commander in the navy and a very distinguished officer; and though Mary, as I have said, only brought me a fortune of 70*l.* a year, and I, as everybody said, in my present position in the office and the city of London, might have reasonably looked out for a lady with much more money, yet my friends agreed that the connection was very respectable, and I was content: as who would not have been with such a darling as Mary? I am sure, for my part, I would not have taken the Lord Mayor's own daughter in place of Mary, even with a plum to her fortune.

Mr. Brough of course was made aware of my approaching marriage, as of everything else relating to every clerk in the office; and I do believe Abednego told him what we had for dinner every day. Indeed, his knowledge of our affairs was wonderful.

He asked me how Mary's money was invested. It was in the three per cent. consols – 2,333*l.* 6*s.* 8*d.*

'Remember,' says he, 'my lad, Mrs. Sam Titmarsh that is to be may have seven per cent. for her money at the very least, and on better security than the Bank of England; for is not a Company of which John Brough is the head better than any other Company in England?' And to be sure I thought he was not far wrong, and promised to speak to Mary's guardians on the subject before our marriage. Lieutenant Smith, her grand-father, had been at the first very much averse to our union. (I must confess that, one day finding me alone with her, and kissing, I believe, the tips of her little fingers, he had taken me by the collar and turned me out of doors.) But Sam Titmarsh, with a salary of 250*l.* a year, a promised fortune of 150*l.* more, and the right-hand man of Mr. John Brough of London, was a very different man from Sam the poor clerk, and the poor clergyman's widow's son; and the old gentleman wrote me a kind letter enough, and begged me to get him six pairs of lamb's-wool stockings and four ditto waistcoats from Romanis', and accepted them too as a present from me when I went down in June – in happy June of 1823 – to fetch my dear Mary away.

Mr. Brough was likewise kindly anxious about my aunt's Slopperton and Squashtail property, which she had not as yet sold, as she talked of doing; and as Mr. B. represented, it was a sin and a shame that any person in whom he took such interest, as he did in all the relatives of his dear young friend, should only have three per cent. for her money, when she could have eight elsewhere. He always called me Sam now, praised me to the other young men (who brought the praises regularly to me), said there was a cover always laid for me at Fulham, and repeatedly took me thither. There was but little company when I went; and M'Whirter used to say he only asked me on days when he had his vulgar acquaintances. But I did not care for the great people, not being born in their sphere; and indeed did not much care for going to the house at all. Miss Belinda was not at all to my liking. After her engagement with Captain Fizgig, and after Mr. Tidd had paid his 20,000l. and Fizgig's great relations had joined in some of our director's companies, Mr. Brough declared he believed that Captain Fizgig's views were mercenary, and put him to the proof at once, by saying that he must take Miss Brough without a farthing, or not have her at all. Whereupon Captain Fizgig got an appointment in the colonies, and Miss Brough became more ill-humoured than ever. But I could not help thinking she was rid of a bad bargain, and pitying poor Tidd, who came back to the charge again more love-sick than ever, and was rebuffed pitilessly by Miss Belinda. Her father plainly told Tidd, too, that his visits were disagreeable to Belinda, and though he must always love and value him, he begged him to discontinue his calls at the Rookery. Poor fellow! he had paid his 20,000l. away for nothing! for what was six per cent. to him compared to six per cent. and the hand of Miss Belinda Brough?

Well, Mr. Brough pitied the poor love-sick swain, as he called me, so much, and felt such a warm sympathy in my

well-being, that he insisted on my going down to Somersetshire with a couple of months' leave: and away I went, as
happy as a lark, with a couple of bran-new suits from Von
Stiltz's in my trunk (I had them made, looking forward to a
certain event), and inside the trunk Lieutenant Smith's fleecy
hosiery; wrapping up a parcel of our prospectuses and two
letters from John Brough, Esq., to my mother our worthy
annuitant, and to Mrs. Hoggarty our excellent shareholder.
Mr. Brough said I was all that the fondest father could wish,
that he considered me as his own boy, and that he earnestly
begged Mrs. Hoggarty not to delay the sale of her little landed
property, as land was high now and *must fall*; whereas the
West Diddlesex Association shares were (comparatively) low,
and must inevitably, in the course of a year or two, double,
treble, quadruple their present value.

In this way I was prepared, and in this way I took leave of
my dear Gus. As we parted in the yard of the Bolt-in-Tun,
Fleet Street, I felt that I never should go back to Salisbury
Square again, and had made my little present to the landlady's
family accordingly. She said I was the respectablest gentleman
she had ever had in her house: nor was that saying much, for
Bell Lane is in the rules of the Fleet, and her lodgers used
commonly to be prisoners on Rule from that place. As for
Gus, the poor fellow cried and blubbered so that he could not
eat a morsel of the muffins and grilled ham with which I
treated him for breakfast in the Bolt-in-Tun coffee-house; and
when I went away was waving his hat and his handkerchief so
in the arch-way of the coach-office, that I do believe the
wheels of the True Blue went over his toes, for I heard him
roaring as we passed through the arch. Ah! how different were
my feelings as I sat proudly there on the box by the side of Jim
Ward, the coachman, to those I had the last time I mounted
that coach, parting from my dear Mary and coming to
London with my DIAMOND-PIN!

When arrived near home (at Grumpley, three miles from
our village, where the True Blue generally stops to take a glass
of ale at the Poppleton Arms) it was as if our Member, Mr.
Poppleton himself was come into the country, so great was
the concourse of people assembled round the inn. And there
was the landlord of the inn and all the people of the village.

Then there was Tom Wheeler, the postboy, from Mrs. Rincer's posting-hotel in our town; he was riding on the old bay posters, and they, heaven bless us! were drawing my aunt's yellow chariot, in which she never went out but thrice in a year, and in which she now sat in her splendid cashmere shawl and a new hat-and-feather. She waved a white handkerchief out of the window, and Tom Wheeler shouted out 'Huzzah!' as did a number of the little blackguard boys of Grumpley: who, to be sure, would huzzah for anything. What a change on Tom Wheeler's part, however! I remembered only a few years before how he had whipped me from the box of the chaise, as I was hanging on for a ride behind.

Next to my aunt's carriage came the four-wheeled chaise of Lieutenant Smith, R.N., who was driving his old fat pony with his lady by his side. I looked in the back seat of the chaise, and felt a little sad at seeing that *Somebody* was not there. But, O silly fellow! there was Somebody in the yellow chariot with my aunt, blushing like a peony, I declare, and looking so happy! – oh, so happy and pretty! She had a white dress, and a light blue and yellow scarf, which my aunt said were the Hoggarty colours; though what the Hoggartys had to do with light blue and yellow, I don't know to this day.

Well, the True Blue guard made a great bellowing on his horn as his four horses dashed away; the boys shouted again; I was placed bodkin between Mrs. Hoggarty and Mary; Tom Wheeler cut into his bays; the lieutenant (who had shaken me cordially by the hand, and whose big dog did not make the slightest attempt at biting me this time) beat his pony till its fat sides lathered again; and thus in this, I may say, unexampled procession, I arrived in triumph at our village.

My dear mother and the girls, – heaven bless them! nine of them in their nankeen spencers (I had something pretty in my trunk for each of them) – could not afford a carriage, but had posted themselves on the road near the village; and there was such a waving of hands and handkerchiefs: and though my aunt did not much notice them, except by a majestic toss of the head, which is pardonable in a woman of her property, yet Mary Smith did even more than I, and waved her hands as much as the whole nine. Ah! how my dear mother cried and blessed me when we met, and called me her soul's comfort and her darling boy, and looked at me as if I were a paragon of virtue and genius: whereas I was only a very lucky young fellow, that by the aid of kind friends had stepped rapidly into a very pretty property.

I was not to stay with my mother, – that had been arranged beforehand; for though she and Mrs. Hoggarty were not remarkably good friends, yet mother said it was for my benefit that I should stay with my aunt, and so gave up the pleasure of having me with her: and though hers was much the humbler house of the two, I need not say I preferred it far to Mrs. Hoggarty's more splendid one; let alone the horrible Rosolio, of which I was obliged now to drink gallons.

It was to Mrs. H.'s then we were driven; she had prepared a great dinner that evening, and hired an extra waiter, and on getting out of the carriage, she gave a sixpence to Tom Wheeler, saying that was for himself, and that she would settle with Mrs. Rincer for the horses afterwards. At which Tom flung the sixpence upon the ground, swore most violently, and was very justly called by my aunt an 'impertinent fellow.'

She had taken such a liking to me that she would hardly bear me out of her sight. We used to sit for morning after morning over her accounts, debating for hours together the propriety of selling the Slopperton property; but no arrangement was come to yet about it, for Hodge and Smithers could not get the price she wanted. And, moreover, she vowed that at her decease she would leave every shilling to me.

Hodge and Smithers, too, gave a grand party, and treated me with marked consideration; as did every single person of the village. Those who could not afford to give dinners gave teas, and all drank the health of the young couple; and many a time after dinner or supper was my Mary made to blush by the allusions to the change in her condition.

The happy day for that ceremony was now fixed, and the 24th July, 1823, saw me the happiest husband of the prettiest girl in Somerset. We were married from my mother's house, who would insist upon that at any rate, and the nine girls acted as bridesmaids; ay! and Gus Hoskins came from town express to be my groomsman, and had my old room at my mother's, and stayed with her for a week, and cast a sheep's-eye upon Miss Winny Titmarsh too, my dear fourth sister, as I afterwards learned.

My aunt was very kind upon the marriage ceremony, indeed. She had desired me some weeks previous to order three magnificent dresses for Mary from the celebrated Madame Mantalini of London, and some elegant trinkets and embroidered pocket-handkerchiefs from Howell and James's. These were sent down to me, and were to be *my* present to the bride; but Mrs. Hoggarty gave me to understand that I need never trouble myself about the payment of the bill and I thought her conduct very generous. Also she lent us her chariot for the wedding-journey, and made with her own hands a beautiful crimson satin reticule for Mrs. Samuel Titmarsh, her dear niece. It contained a huswife completely furnished with needles, &c., for she hoped Mrs. Titmarsh would never neglect her needle; and a purse containing some silver pennies, and a very curious pocket-piece. 'As long as you keep these, my dear,' said Mrs. Hoggarty, 'you will never want; and fervently – fervently do I pray that you will keep them.' In the carriage-pocket we found a paper of biscuits and a bottle of Rosolio. We laughed at this, and made it over to Tom Wheeler – who, however, did not seem to like it much better than we.

I need not say I was married in Mr. Von Stiltz's coat (the third and fourth coats, heaven help us! in a year), and that I wore sparkling in my bosom the GREAT HOGGARTY DIAMOND.

CHAPTER IX

BRINGS BACK SAM, HIS WIFE, AUNT, AND DIAMOND, TO LONDON

We pleased ourselves during the honeymoon with forming plans for our life in London, and a pretty paradise did we build for ourselves! Well, we were but forty years old between us; and, for my part, I never found any harm come of castle-building, but a great deal of pleasure.

Before I left London I had, to say the truth, looked round me for a proper place, befitting persons of our small income; and Gus Hoskins and I, who hunted after office-hours in couples, had fixed on a very snug little cottage in Camden Town, where there was a garden that certain *small people* might play in when they came: a horse and gig-house, if ever we kept one, – and why not, in a few years? – and a fine healthy air, at a reasonable distance from 'Change; all for 30*l.* a year. I had described this little spot to Mary as enthusiastically as Sancho describes Lizias to Don Quixote; and my dear wife was delighted with the prospect of housekeeping there, vowed she would cook all the best dishes herself (especially jam-pudding, of which I confess I am very fond), and promised Gus that he should dine with us at Clematis Bower every Sunday; only he must not smoke those horrid cigars. As for Gus, he vowed he would have a room in the neighbour-hood too, for he could not bear to go back to Bell Lane, where we two had been so happy together; and so good-natured Mary said she would ask my sister Winny to come and keep her company. At which Hoskins blushed, and said, 'Pooh! nonsense now.'

But all our hopes of a happy, snug Clematis Lodge were dashed to the ground on our return from our little honey-moon excursion; when Mrs. Hoggarty informed us that she was sick of the country, and was determined to go to London with her dear nephew and niece, and keep house for them, and introduce them to her friends in the metropolis.

What could we do? We wished her at – Bath, certainly not in London. But there was no help for it; and we were obliged to bring her: for, as my mother said, if we offended her, her fortune would go out of our family; and were we two young people not likely to want it?

So we came to town rather dismally in the carriage, posting the whole way; for the carriage must be brought, and a person of my aunt's rank in life could not travel by the stage. And I had to pay 14l. for the posters, which pretty nearly exhausted all my little hoard of cash.

First we went into lodgings – into three sets in three weeks. We quarrelled with the first landlady, because my aunt vowed that she cut a slice of the leg of mutton which was served for our dinner; from the second lodgings we went because aunt vowed the maid would steal the candles; from the third we went because aunt Hoggarty came down to breakfast the morning after our arrival with her face shockingly swelled and bitten by – never mind what. To cut a long tale short, I was half mad with the continual choppings and changings, and the long stories and scoldings of my aunt. As for her great acquaintances, none of them were in London; and she made it a matter of quarrel with me that I had not introduced her to John Brough, Esquire, M.P., and to Lord and Lady Tiptoff, her relatives.

Mr. Brough was at Brighton when we arrived in town; and on his return I did not care at first to tell our director that I had brought my aunt with me, or mention my embarrassments for money. He looked rather serious when perforce I spoke of the latter to him and asked for an advance; but when he heard that my lack of money had been occasioned by the bringing of my aunt to London, his tone instantly changed. 'That, my dear boy, alters the question; Mrs. Hoggarty is of an age when all things must be yielded to her. Here are a hundred pounds; and I beg you to draw upon me whenever you are in the least in want of money.' This gave me breathing-time until she should pay her share of the household expenses. And the very next day Mr. and Mrs. John Brough, in their splendid carriage-and-four, called upon Mrs. Hoggarty and my wife at our lodgings in Lamb's Conduit Street.

It was on the very day when my poor aunt appeared with her face in that sad condition; and she did not fail to inform Mrs. Brough of the cause, and to state that at Castle Hoggarty, or at her country place in Somersetshire, she had never heard or thought of such vile, odious things.

'Gracious heavens!' shouted John Brough, Esquire, 'a lady of your rank to suffer in this way! – the excellent relative of my dear boy, Titmarsh! Never, madam – never let it be said that Mrs. Hoggarty of Castle Hoggarty should be subject to such horrible humiliation, while John Brough has a home to offer her – a humble, happy, Christian home, madam; though unlike, perhaps, the splendour to which you have been accustomed in the course of your distinguished career. Isabella my love! – Belinda! speak to Miss Hoggarty. Tell her that John Brough's house is hers from garret to cellar. I repeat it, madam, from garret to cellar. I desire – I insist – I order, that Mrs. Hoggarty of Castle Hoggarty's trunks should be placed this instant in my carriage! Have the goodness to look to them yourself, Mrs. Titmarsh, and see that your dear aunt's comforts are better provided for than they have been.'

Mary went away rather wondering at this order. But, to be sure, Mr. Brough was a great man, and her Samuel's benefactor; and though the silly child absolutely began to cry as she packed and toiled at aunt's enormous valises, yet she performed the work, and came down with a smiling face to my aunt, who was entertaining Mr. and Mrs. Brough with a long and particular account of the balls at the Castle, in Dublin, in Lord Charleville's time.

'I have packed the trunks, aunt, but I am not strong enough to bring them down,' said Mary.

'Certainly not, certainly not,' said John Brough, perhaps a little ashamed. Hallo! George, Frederic, Augustus, come upstairs this instant, and bring down the trunks of Mrs. Hoggarty of Castle Hoggarty, which this young lady will show you.'

Nay, so great was Mr. Brough's condescension, that when some of his fashionable servants refused to meddle with the trunks, he himself seized a pair of them with both hands, carried them to the carriage, and shouted loud enough for all Lamb's Conduit Street to hear, 'John Brough is not proud –

no, no; and if his footmen are too high and mighty, he'll show them a lesson of humility.'

Mrs. Brough was for running downstairs too, and taking the trunks from her husband; but they were too heavy for her, so she contented herself with sitting on one, and asking all persons who passed her, whether John Brough was not an angel of a man?

In this way it was that my aunt left us. I was not aware of her departure, for I was at the office at the time; and strolling back at five with Gus, saw my dear Mary smiling and bobbing from the window, and beckoning to us both to come up. This I thought was very strange, because Mrs. Hoggarty could not abide Hoskins, and indeed had told me repeatedly that either she or he must quit the house. Well, we went upstairs, and there was Mary, who had dried her tears and received us with the most smiling of faces, and laughed and clapped her hands, and danced, and shook Gus's hand. And what do you think the little rogue proposed? I am blest if she did not say she would like to go to Vauxhall!

As dinner was laid for three persons only, Gus took his seat with fear and trembling; and then Mrs. Sam Titmarsh related the circumstances which had occurred, and how Mrs. Hoggarty had been whisked away to Fulham in Mr. Brough's splendid carriage-and-four, 'Let her go,' I am sorry to say, said I; and indeed we relished our veal-cutlets and jam-pudding a great deal more than Mrs. Hoggarty did her dinner off plate at the Rookery.

We had a very merry party to Vauxhall, Gus insisting on standing treat; and you may be certain that my aunt, whose absence was prolonged for three weeks, was heartily welcome to remain away, for we were much merrier and more comfortable without her. My little Mary used to make my breakfast before I went to office of mornings; and on Sundays we had a holiday, and saw the dear little children eat their boiled beef and potatoes at the Foundling, and heard the beautiful music: but, beautiful as it is, I think the children were a more beautiful sight still, and the look of their innocent happy faces was better than the best sermon. On week-days Mrs. Titmarsh would take a walk about five o'clock in the evening, on the *left*-hand side of Lamb's Conduit Street (as

you go to Holborn) – ay, and sometimes pursue her walk as
far as Snow Hill, when two young gents from the I.W.D. Fire
and Life were pretty sure to meet her; and then how happily
we all trudged off to dinner! Once we came up as a monster of
a man, with high heels and a gold-headed cane, and whiskers
all over his face, was grinning under Mary's bonnet, and
chattering to her, close to Day and Martin's Blacking Manufactory (not near such a handsome thing then as it is now) –
there was the man chattering and ogling his best, when who
should come up but Gus and I? And in the twinkling of a
pegpost, as Lord Duberley says, my gentleman was seized by
the collar of his coat and found himself sprawling under a
stand of hackney-coaches; where all the watermen were
grinning at him. The best of it was, he left his *head of hair and
whiskers* in my hand: but Mary said, 'Don't be hard upon him,
Samuel; it's only a Frenchman.' And so we gave him his wig
back, which one of the grinning stable-boys put on and
carried to him as he lay in the straw.

He shrieked out something about 'arrêtez,' and 'Français,'
and 'champ-d'honneur;' but we walked on, Gus putting his
thumb to his nose and stretching out his finger at Master
Frenchman. This made everybody laugh; and so the adventure
ended.

About ten days after my aunt's departure came a letter from
her, of which I give a copy: –

'MY DEAR NEPHEW, – It was my earnest whish e'er this to
have returned to London, where I am sure you and my
niece Titmarsh miss me very much, and where she, poor
thing, quite inexperienced in the ways of 'the great metro-
pulus,' in aconamy, and indeed in every qualaty requasit in
a good wife and the mistress of a famaly, can hardly
manidge, I am sure, without me.

'Tell her *on no account* to pay more than 6½d. for the prime
pieces, 4¾d. for soup meat; and that the very best of London
butter is to be had for 8½d.; of course, for pudns and the
kitchin you'll employ a commoner sort. My trunks were
sadly packed by Mrs. Titmarsh, and the hasp of the
portmantyoulock has gone through my yellow satn. I have
darned it, and woar it already twice, at two ellygant

(though quiat) evening parties given by my *hospatable* host; and my pegreen velvet on Saturday at a grand dinner, when Lord Scaramouch handed me to table. Everything was in the most *sumptious style*. Soup top and bottom (white and brown), removed by turbit and sammon with *immense boles of lobster-sauce*. Lobsters alone cost 15*s*. Turbit, three guineas. The hole sammon, weighing, I'm sure, 15lbs., and *never seen* at table again; not a bitt of pickled sammon the hole weak afterwards. This kind of extravagance would *just suit* Mrs. Sam Titmarsh, who, as I always say, burns *the candle at both ends*. Well, young people, it is lucky for you you have an old aunt who knows better, and has a long purse; without witch, I daresay, *some* folks would be glad to see her out of doors. I don't mean you, Samuel, who have, I must say, been a dutiful nephew to me. Well, I daresay I shan't live long, and some folks won't be sorry to have me in my grave.

'Indeed, on Sunday I was taken in my stomick very ill, and thought it might have been the lobster-sauce; but Dr. Blogg, who was called in, said it was, he very much feared, *cumsumptive*; but gave me some pills and a draft w^h made me better. Please call upon him – he lives at Pimlico, and you can walk out there after office hours – and present him with 1*l*. 1*s*., with my compliments. I have no money here but a 10*l*. note, the rest being locked up in my box at Lamb's Cundit Street.

'Although the flesh is not neglected in Mr. B.'s sumptious establishment, I can assure you the *sperrit* is likewise cared for. Mr. B. reads and igspounds every morning; and o but his exorcises refresh the hungry sole before breakfast! Everything is in the handsomest style – silver and goold plate at breakfast, lunch, and dinner; and his crest and motty, a behive, with the Latn word *Industria*, meaning industry, on *everything* – even on the chany juggs and things in my bedd-room. On Sunday we were favoured by a special outpouring from the Rev. Grimes Wapshot, of the Amabaptist Congriation here, and who egshorted for 3 hours in the afternoon in Mr. B's private chapel. As the widow of a Hoggarty, I have always been a staunch supporter of the established Church of England and Ireland;

but I must say Mr. Wapshot's stirring way was far superior to that of the Rev. Bland Blenkinsop of the Establishment, who lifted up his voice after dinner for a short
discourse of two hours.

'Mrs. Brough is, between ourselves, a poor creature,
and has no sperrit of her own. As for Miss B., she is so
saucy that once I promised to box her years; and would
have left the house, had not Mr. B. taken my part, and
Miss made me a suitable appolojy.

'I don't know when I shall return to town, being made
really so welcome here. Doctor Blogg says the air of
Fulham is the best in the world for my simtums; and as the
ladies of the house do not choose to walk out with me, the
Rev. Grimes Wapshot has often been kind enough to lend
me his arm, and 'tis sweet with such a guide to wander
both to Putney and Wandsworth, and igsamin the wonderful works of nature. I have spoke to him about the
Slopperton property, and he is not of Mr. B.'s opinion
that I should sell it: but on this point I shall follow my
own counsel.

'Meantime you must gett into more comfortable lodgings, and lett my bedd be warmed every night, and of
rainy days have a fire in the grate; and let Mrs. Titmarsh
look up my blue silk dress, and turn it against I come; and
there is my purple spencer she can have for herself; and I
hope she does not wear those three splendid gowns you
gave her, but keep them until *better times*. I shall soon
introduse her to my friend Mr. Brough, and others of my
acquaintances; and am always   'Your loving AUNT.

'I have ordered a chest of the Rosolio to be sent from
Somersetshire. When it comes, please to send half down
here (paying the carriage, of course). 'Twill be an accept-
able present to my kind entertainer, Mr. B.'

This letter was brought to me by Mr. Brough himself at
the office, who apologized to me for having broken the seal
by inadvertence; for the letter had been mingled with some
more of his own, and he opened it without looking at the
superscription. Of course he had not read it and I was glad of

that; for I should not have liked him to see my aunt's opinion of his daughter and lady.

The next day, a gentleman at 'Tom's Coffee-house,' Cornhill, sent me word at the office that he wanted particularly to speak to me: and I stepped thither, and found my old friend Smithers, of the house of Hodge and Smithers, just off the coach, with his carpet-bag between his legs.

'Sam my boy,' said he, 'you are your aunt's heir, and I have a piece of news for you regarding her property which you ought to know. She wrote us down a letter for a chest of that home-make wine of hers which she calls Rosolio, and which lies in our warehouse along with her furniture.'

'Well,' says, I, smiling, 'she may part with as much Rosolio as she likes for me. I cede all my right.'

'Psha!' says Smithers, 'it's not that; though her furniture puts us to a deuced inconvenience, to be sure – it's not that: but, in the postscript of her letter, she orders us to advertise the Slopperton and Squashtail estates for immediate sale, as she purposes placing her capital elsewhere.'

I knew that the Slopperton and Squashtail property had been the source of a very pretty income to Messrs. Hodge and Smithers, for aunt was always at law with her tenants, and paid dearly for her litigious spirit; so that Mr. Smither's concern regarding the sale of it did not seem to me to be quite disinterested.

'And did you come to London, Mr. Smithers, expressly to acquaint me with this fact? It seems to me you had much better have obeyed my aunt's instructions at once, or go to her at Fulham, and consult with her on this subject.'

''Sdeath, Mr. Titmarsh! don't you see that if she makes a sale of her property, she will hand over the money to Brough; and if Brough gets the money he – '

'Will give her seven per cent. for it instead of three, – there's no harm in that.'

'But there's such a thing as security, look you. He is a warm man, certainly – very warm – quite respectable – most undoubtedly respectable. But who knows? A panic may take place; and then these five hundred companies in which he is engaged may bring him to ruin. There's the Ginger Beer Company, of which Brough is a director: awkward reports are abroad concerning it. The Consolidated Baffin's Bay Muff and Tippet Company – the shares are down very low, and Brough is a director there. The Patent Pump Company – shares at 65, and a fresh call, which nobody will pay.'

'Nonsense, Mr. Smithers! Has not Mr. Brough five hundred thousand pounds' worth of shares in the INDEPENDENT WEST DIDDLESEX, and is THAT at a discount? Who recommended my aunt to invest her money in that speculation, I should like to know?' I had him there.

'Well, well, it is a very good speculation, certainly, and has brought you three hundred a year, Sam my boy; and you may thank us for the interest we took in you (indeed, we loved you as a son, and Miss Hodge has not recovered from a certain marriage yet). You don't intend to rebuke us for making your fortune, do you?'

'No, hang it, no!' says I, and shook hands with him, and accepted a glass of sherry and biscuits, which he ordered forthwith.

Smithers returned, however, to the charge. – 'Sam,' he said, 'mark my words, and *take your aunt away from the Rookery*. She wrote to Mrs. S. a long account of a reverend gent with whom she walks out there, – the Rev. Grimes Wapshot. That man has an eye upon her. He was tried at Lancaster in the year '14 for forgery, and narrowly escaped with his neck. Have a care of him – he has an eye to her money.'

'Nay,' said I, taking out Mrs. Hoggarty's letter: 'read for yourself.'

He read it over very carefully, seemed to be amused by it; and as he returned it to me, 'Well Sam,' he said, 'I have only two favours to ask of you: one is, not to mention that I am in town to any living soul; and the other is to give me a dinner in Lamb's Conduit Street with your pretty wife.'

'I promise you both gladly,' I said, laughing. 'But if you dine with us, your arrival in town must be known, for my friend Gus Hoskins dines with us likewise; and has done so nearly every day since my aunt went.'

He laughed too, and said, 'We must swear Gus to secrecy over a bottle.' And so we parted till dinner-time.

The indefatigable lawyer pursued his attack after dinner, and was supported by Gus and by my wife too; who certainly was disinterested in the matter – more than disinterested, for she would have given a great deal to be spared my aunt's company. But she said she saw the force of Mr. Smither's arguments, and I admitted their justice with a sigh. However, I rode my high horse, and vowed that my aunt should do what she liked with her money; and that I was not the man who would influence her in any way in the disposal of it.

After tea, the two gents walked away together, and Gus told me that Smithers had asked him a thousand questions about the office, about Brough, about me and my wife, and everything concerning us. 'You are a lucky fellow, Mr. Hoskins, and seem to be the friend of this charming young couple,' said Smithers; and Gus confessed he was, and said he had dined with us fifteen times in six weeks, and that a better and more hospitable fellow than I did not exist. This I state not to trumpet my own praises, – no, no; but because these questions of Smithers's had a good deal to do with the subsequent events narrated in this little history.

Being seated at dinner the next day off the cold leg of mutton that Smithers had admired so the day before, and Gus as usual having his legs under our mahogany, a hackney-coach drove up to the door, which we did not much heed; a step was heard on the floor, which we hoped might be for the two-pair lodger, when who should burst into the room but Mrs. Hoggarty herself! Gus, who was blowing the froth off a pot of porter preparatory to a delicious drink of the beverage, and had been making us die of laughing with his stories and jokes, laid down the pewter pot as Mrs. H. came in, and looked quite sick and pale. Indeed we all felt a little uneasy.

My aunt looked haughtily in Mary's face, then fiercely at Gus, and saying, 'It is too true – my poor boy – *already!* ' flung herelf hysterically into my arms, and swore, almost choking, that she would never, never leave me.

I could not understand the meaning of this extraordinary agitation on Mrs. Hoggarty's part, nor could any of us. She refused Mary's hand when the poor thing rather nervously offered it; and when Gus timidly said, 'I think, Sam, I'm rather in the way here, and perhaps – had better go.' Mrs. H. looked him full in the face, pointed to the door majestically with her forefinger, and said, 'I think, sir you *had* better go.'

'I hope Mr. Hoskins will stay as long as he pleases,' said my wife, with spirit.

'*Of course* you hope so, madam,' answered Mrs. Hoggarty, very sarcastic. But Mary's speech and my aunt's were quite lost upon Gus; for he had instantly run to his hat, and I heard him tumbling downstairs.

The quarrel ended as usually, by Mary's bursting into a fit of tears, and by my aunt's repeating the assertion that it was not too late, she trusted; and from that day forth she would never, never leave me.

'What could have made aunt return and be so angry?' said I to Mary that night, as we were in our own room; but my wife protested she did not know: and it was only some time after that I found out the reason of this quarrel, and of Mrs. H.'s sudden reappearance.

The horrible, fat, coarse little Smithers told me the matter as a very good joke, only the other year, when he showed me the letter of Hickson, Dixon, Paxton and Jackson, which has before been quoted in my Memoirs.

'Sam my boy,' said he, 'you were determined to leave Mrs. Hoggarty in Brough's clutches at the Rookery, and I was determined to have her away. I resolved to kill two of your mortal enemies with one stone as it were. It was quite clear to me that the Rev. Grimes Wapshot had an eye to your aunt's fortune; and Mr. Brough had similar predatory intentions regarding her. Predatory is a mild word, Sam; if I had said robbery at once, I should express my meaning clearer.

'Well, I took the Fulham stage, and, arriving, made straight for the lodgings of the reverend gentleman, "Sir," said I, on finding that worthy gent, – he was drinking warm brandy-and-water, Sam, at two o'clock in the day or at least the room smelt very strongly of that beverage – "Sir," says I, "you were tried for forgery in the year '14, at Lancaster assizes."

'"And acquitted, sir. My innocence was by Providence made clear," said Wapshot.

'"But you were not acquitted of embezzlement in '16, sir," says I, "and passed two years in York gaol in consequence." I knew the fellow's history, for I had a writ out against him when he was a preacher at Clifton. I followed up my blow. "Mr. Wapshot," said I, "you are making love to an excellent

lady now at the house of Mr. Brough; if you do not promise
to give up all pursuit of her, I will expose you."

"'I *have* promised," said Wapshot, rather surprised, and
looking more easy. "I have given my solemn promise to Mr.
Brough, who was with me this very morning, storming, and
scolding, and swearing. Oh, sir, it would have frightened you
to hear a Christian babe like him swear as he did."

"'Mr. Brough been here?" says I, rather astonished.

"'Yes; I suppose you are both here on the same scent," says
Wapshot. "You want to marry the widow with the Slopperton and Squashtail estate, do you? Well, well, have your way.
I've promised not to have anything more to do with the
widow, and a Wapshot's honour is sacred."

"'I suppose, sir," says I, "Mr. Brough has threatened to kick
you out of doors if you call again?"

"'You *have* been with him, I see," says the reverend gent,
with a shrug: then I remembered what you had told me of the
broken seal of your letter, and have not the slightest doubt
that Brough opened and read every word of it.

'Well, the first bird was bagged: both I and Brough had had
a shot at him. Now I had to fire at the whole Rookery; and off
I went, primed and loaded, sir, – primed and loaded.

'It was past eight when I arrived, and I saw, after I passed
the lodge-gates, a figure that I knew, walking in the shrubbery
–that of your respected aunt, sir: but I wished to meet the
amiable ladies of the house before I saw her; because look,
friend Titmarsh, I saw by Mrs. Hoggarty's letter, that she and
they were at daggers drawn, and hoped to get her out of the
house at once by means of a quarrel with them.'

I laughed, and owned that Mr. Smithers was a very cunning
fellow.

'As luck would have it,' continued he, 'Miss Brough was in
the drawing-room twangling on a guitar, and singing most
atrociously out of tune; but as I entered at the door, I cried
"Hush!" to the footman, as loud as possible, stood stock-still,
and then walked forward on tiptoe lightly. Miss B. could see
in the glass every movement that I made; she pretended not to
see, however, and finished the song with a regular roulade.

"'Gracious heaven!" said I, "do, madam, pardon me for
interrupting that delicious harmony, – for coming unaware

upon it, for daring uninvited to listen to it."

"'Do you come for mamma, sir?" said Miss Brough, with as much graciousness as her physiognomy could command. "I am Miss Brough, sir."

"'I wish, madam, you would let me not breathe a word regarding my business until you have sung another charming strain."

'She did not sing, but looked pleased, and said, "La! sir, what is your business?"

"'My business is with a lady, your respected father's guest in this house."

"'Oh, Mrs. Hoggarty!" says Miss Brough, flouncing towards the bell, and ringing it. "John, send to Mrs. Hoggarty, in the shrubbery; here is a gentleman who wants to see her."

"'I know," continued I, "Mrs. Hoggarty's peculiarities as well as any one, madam; and aware that those and her education are not such as to make her a fit companion for you, I know you do not like her; she has written to us in Somersetshire that you do not like her."

"'What! she has been abusing us to our friends, has she?" cried Miss Brough (it was the very point I wished to insinuate). "If she does not like us, why does she not leave us?"

"'She *has* made rather a long visit," said I; "and I am sure that her nephew and niece are longing for her return. Pray, madam, do not move, for you may aid me in the object for which I come."

'The object for which I came, sir, was to establish a regular battle-royal between the two ladies; at the end of which I intended to appeal to Mrs. Hoggarty, and say that she ought really no longer to stay in a house with the members of which she had such unhappy differences. Well, sir, the battle-royal was fought, – Miss Belinda opening the fire, by saying she understood Mrs. Hoggarty had been calumniating her to her friends. But though at the end of it Miss rushed out of the room in a rage, and vowed she would leave her home unless that odious woman left it, your dear aunt said, "Ha, ha! I know the minx's vile stratagems; but thank heaven! I have a good heart, and my religion enables me to forgive her. I shall not leave her excellent papa's house, or vex by my departure that worthy, admirable man."

'I then tried Mrs. H. on the score of compassion. "Your niece," said I, "Mrs. Titmarsh, madam, has been of late, Sam says, rather poorly, – qualmish of mornings, madam, – a little nervous, and low in spirits, – symptoms, madam, that are scarcely to be mistaken in a young married person."

'Mrs. Hoggarty said she had an admirable cordial that she would send Mrs. Samuel Titmarsh, and she was perfectly certain it would do her good.

'With very great unwillingness I was obliged now to bring my last reserve into the field, and may tell you what that was, Sam my boy, now that the matter is so long passed. "Madam," said I, "there's a matter about which I must speak, though indeed I scarcely dare. I dined with your nephew yesterday, and met at his table a young man – a young man of low manners, but evidently one who has blinded your nephew, and I too much fear has succeeded in making an impression upon your niece. His name is Hoskins, madam; and when I state that he who was never in the house during your presence there, has dined with your too-confiding nephew sixteen times in three weeks, I may leave you to imagine what I dare not – dare not imagine myself."

'The shot told. Your aunt bounced up at once, and in ten minutes more was in my carriage, on our way back to London. There, sir, was not *that* generalship?'

'And you played this pretty trick off at my wife's expense, Mr. Smithers?' said I.

'At your wife's expense, certainly; but for the benefit of both of you.'

'It's lucky, sir, that you are an old man,' I replied, 'and that the affair happened ten years ago; or, by the Lord, Mr. Smithers, I would have given you such a horsewhipping as you never heard of!'

But this was the way in which Mrs. Hoggarty was brought back to her relatives; and this was the reason why we took that house in Bernard Street, the doings at which must now be described.

CHAPTER X

OF SAM'S PRIVATE AFFAIRS, AND OF
THE FIRM OF BROUGH AND HOFF

We took a genteel house in Bernard Street, Russell Square, and my aunt sent for all her furniture from the country; which would have filled two such houses, but which came pretty cheap to us young housekeepers, as we had only to pay the carriage of the goods from Bristol.

When I brought Mrs. H. her third half-year's dividend, having not for four months touched a shilling of her money, I must say she gave me 50*l.* of the 80*l.*, and told me that was ample pay for the board and lodging of a poor old woman like her, who did not eat more than a sparrow.

I have myself, in the country, seen her eat nine sparrows in a pudding; but she was rich, and I could not complain. If she saved 600*l.* a year, at the least, by living with us, why, all the savings would one day come to me; and so Mary and I consoled ourselves, and tried to manage matters as well as we might. It was no easy task to keep a mansion in Bernard Street and save money out of 470*l.* a year, which was my income. But what a lucky fellow I was to have such an income!

As Mrs. Hoggarty left the Rookery in Smithers's carriage, Mr. Brough, with his four greys, was entering the lodge-gate; and I should like to have seen the looks of these two gentlemen, as the one was carrying the other's prey off, out of his own very den, under his very nose.

He came to see her the next day, and protested that he would not leave the house until she left it with him: that he had heard of his daughter's infamous conduct, and had seen her in tears – 'in tears, madam, and on her knees, imploring heaven to pardon her!' But Mr. B. was obliged to leave the house without my aunt, who had a *causa major* for staying, and hardly allowed poor Mary out of her sight, – opening every one of the letters that came into the house directed to my wife, and suspecting hers to everybody. Mary never told me of all this pain for many, many years afterwards; but had always a smiling face for her husband when he came home from his work. As for poor Gus, my aunt had so frightened him, that he never once showed his nose in the place all the time we lived there; but used to be content with news of Mary, of whom he was as fond as he was of me.

Mr. Brough, when my aunt left him, was in a furious ill-humour with me. He found fault with me ten times a day, and openly, before the gents of the office; but I let him one day know pretty smartly that I was not only a servant, but a considerable shareholder in the company; that I defied him to find fault with my work or my regularity; and that I was not minded to receive any insolent language from him or any man. He said it was always so; that he had never cherished a young man in his bosom, but the ingrate had turned on him; that he was accustomed to wrong and undutifulness from his children, and that he would pray that the sin might be forgiven me. A moment before he had been cursing and swearing at me, and speaking to me as if I had been his shoeblack. But, look you, I was not going to put up with any more of Madam Brough's airs, or of his. With *me* they might act as they thought fit; but I did not choose that my wife should be passed over by them, as she had been in the matter of the visit to Fulham.

Brough ended by warning me of Hodge and Smithers. 'Beware of these men,' said he; 'but for my honesty, your aunt's landed property would have been sacrificed by these cormorants: and when, for her benefit – which you, obstinate young man, will not perceive – I wished to dispose of her land, her attorneys actually had the audacity – the unchristian avarice I may say – to ask ten per cent. commission on the sale.'

There might be some truth in this, I thought; at any rate, when rogues fall out, honest men come by their own: and now I began to suspect, I am sorry to say, that both the attorney and the director had a little of the rogue in their composition. It was especially about my wife's fortune that Mr. B. showed *his* cloven foot; for proposing, as usual, that I should purchase shares with it in our company, I told him that my wife was a minor, and as such her little fortune was vested out of my control altogether. He flung away in a rage at this; and I soon saw that he did not care for me any more, by Abednego's manner to me. No more holidays, no more advances of money, had I; on the contrary, the private clerkship at 50*l*. was abolished, and I found myself on my 250*l*. a year again. Well, what then? it was always a good income, and I did my duty, and laughed at the director.

About this time, in the beginning of 1824, the Jamaica Ginger Beer Company shut up shop – exploded, as Gus said, with a bang! The Patent Pump shares were down to 15*l*. upon a paid-up capital of 65*l*. Still ours were at a high premium; and the Independent West Diddlesex held its head up as proudly as any office in London. Roundhand's abuse had had some influence against the director, certainly; for he hinted at malversation of shares: but the company still stood as united as the Hand-in-Hand, and as firm as the Rock.

To return to the state of affairs in Bernard Street, Russell Square: My aunt's old furniture crammed our little rooms; and my aunt's enormous old jingling grand piano, with crooked legs and half the strings broken, occupied three-fourths of the little drawing-room. Here used Mrs. H. to sit, and play us, for hours, sonatas that were in fashion in Lord Charleville's time; and sung with a cracked voice, till it was all that we could do to refrain from laughing.

And it was queer to remark the change that had taken place in Mrs. Hoggarty's character now: for whereas she was in the country among the topping persons of the village, and quite content with a tea-party at six and a game of twopenny whist afterwards, – in London she would never dine till seven; would have a fly from the mews to drive in the Park twice a week; cut and uncut, and ripped up and twisted over and over, all her old gowns, flounces, caps, and fallals, and kept my poor Mary from morning till night altering them to the present mode. Mrs. Hoggarty, moreover, appeared in a new wig; and, I am sorry to say, turned out with such a pair of red cheeks as Nature never gave her, and as made all the people in Bernard Street stare, where they are not as yet used to such fashions.

Moreover, she insisted upon our establishing a servant in livery, – a boy, that is, of about sixteen, – who was dressed in one of the old liveries that she had brought with her from Somersetshire, decorated with new cuffs and collars, and new buttons; on the latter were represented the united crests of the Titmarshes and Hoggarties, viz. a tomtit rampant and a hog in armour. I thought this livery and crest-button rather absurd, I must confess; though my family *is* very ancient. And heavens! what a roar of laughter was raised in the office one day, when the little servant in the big livery, with the immense cane, walked in and brought me a message from Mrs. Hoggarty of Castle Hoggarty! Furthermore, all letters were delivered on a silver tray. If we had had a baby, I believe aunt would have had it down on the tray: but there was as yet no foundation for Mr. Smithers's insinuation upon that score, any more than for his other cowardly fabrication before narrated. Aunt and Mary used to walk gravely up and down the New Road, with the boy following with his great gold-headed stick; but though there was all this ceremony and parade, and aunt still talked of her acquaintances, we did not see a single person from week's end to week's end, and a more dismal house than ours could hardly be found in London town.

On Sundays, Mrs. Hoggarty used to go to Saint Pancras Church, then just built, and as handsome as Covent Garden Theatre; and of evenings, to a meeting-house of the Anabaptists; and *that* day, at least, Mary and I had to ourselves, – for we chose to have seats at the Foundling, and heard the charming music there, and my wife used to look wistfully in the pretty children's faces, – and so, for the matter of that, did I. It was not, however, till a year after our marriage that she spoke in a way which shall be here passed over, but which filled both her and me with inexpressible joy.

I remember she had the news to give me on the very day when the Muff and Tippet Company shut up, after swallowing a capital of 300,000*l.*, as some said, and nothing to show for it except a treaty with some Indians, who had afterwards tomahawked the agent of the company. Some people said there were no Indians, and no agent to be tomahawked at all; but that the whole had been invented in a house in Crutched Friars. Well, I pitied poor Tidd, whose 20,000*l.* were thus gone in a year, and whom I met in the city that day with a most ghastly face. He had 1,000*l.* of debts, he said, and talked of shooting himself; but he was only arrested, and passed a long time in the Fleet. Mary's delightful news, however, soon put Tidd and the Muff and Tippet Company out of my head: as you may fancy.

Other circumstances now occurred in the city of London which seemed to show that our director was – what is not to be found in Johnson's 'Dictionary' – rather shaky. Three of his companies had broken; four more were in a notoriously insolvent state; and even at the meetings of the directors of the West Diddlesex, some stormy words passed, which ended in the retirement of several of the board. Friends of Mr. B.'s filled up their places; Mr. Puppet, Mr. Straw, Mr. Query, and other respectable gents coming forward and joining the concern. Brough and Hoff dissolved partnership; and Mr. B. said he had quite enough to do to manage the I. W. D., and intended gradually to retire from the other affairs. Indeed, such an association as ours was enough work for any man, let alone the parliamentary duties which Brough was called on to perform, and the seventy-two law-suits which burst upon him as principal director of the late companies.

Perhaps I should here describe the desperate attempt made by Mrs. Hoggarty to introduce herself into genteel life. Strange to say, although we had my Lord Tiptoff's word to the contrary, she insisted upon it that she and Lady Drum were intimately related; and no sooner did she read in the *Morning Post* of the arrival of her ladyship and her granddaughters in London, than she ordered the fly before mentioned, and left cards to their respective houses; her card that is – 'MRS HOGGARTY of CASTLE HOGGARTY' magnificently engraved in Gothic letters and flourishes; and ours, viz. 'Mr. and Mrs. S. Titmarsh,' which she had printed for the purpose.

She would have stormed Lady Jane Preston's door and forced her way upstairs, in spite of Mary's entreaties to the contrary, had the footman who received her card given her the least encouragement; but that functionary, no doubt struck by the oddity of her appearance placed himself in the front of the door, and declared that he had positive orders not to admit any strangers to his lady. On which Mrs. Hoggarty clenched her fist out of the coach-window, and promised that she would have him turned away.

Yellowplush only burst out laughing at this; and though aunt wrote a most indignant letter to Mr. Edmund Preston, complaining of the insolence of the servants of that right honourable gent, Mr. Preston did not take any notice of her letter, further than to return it, with a desire that he might not be troubled with such impertinent visits for the future. A pretty day we had of it when this letter arrived, owing to my aunt's disappointment and rage in reading the contents, for when Solomon brought up the note on the silver tea-tray as usual, my aunt seing Mr. Preston's seal and name at the corner of the letter (which is the common way of writing adopted by those official gents) – my aunt, I say, seeing his name and seal, cried, 'Now, Mary, who is right?' and betted my wife a sixpence that the envelope contained an invitation to dinner. She never paid the sixpence, though she lost, but contented herself by abusing Mary all day, and said I was a poor-spirited sneak for not instantly horse-whipping Mr. P. A pretty joke, indeed! They would have hanged me in those days, as they did the man who shot Mr. Perceval.

And now I should be glad to enlarge upon that experience in genteel life which I obtained through the perseverance of Mrs. Hoggarty; but it must be owned that my opportunities were but few, lasting only for the brief period of six months: and also, genteel society has been fully described already by various authors of novels, whose names need not here be set down, but who, being themselves connected with the aristocracy, viz. as members of noble families, or as footmen or hangers-on thereof, naturally understand their subject a great deal better than a poor young fellow from a fire office can.

There was our celebrated adventure in the Opera House, whither Mrs. H. would insist upon conducting us; and where, in a room of the establishment called the crush-room, where the ladies and gents after the music and dancing await the arrival of their carriages (a pretty figure did our little Solomon cut by the way, with his big cane, among the gentlemen of the shoulder-knot assembled in the lobby!) – where, I say, in the crush-room, Mrs. H. rushed up to old Lady Drum, whom I pointed out to her, and insisted upon claiming relationship with her ladyship. But my Lady Drum had only a memory when she chose, as I may say, and had entirely on this occasion thought fit to forget her connection with the Titmarshes and Hoggarties. Far from recognizing us, indeed, she called Mrs. Hoggarty an 'ojus 'oman,' and screamed out as loud as possible for a police-officer.

This and other rebuffs made my aunt perceive the vanities of this wicked world, as she said, and threw her more and more into really serious society. She formed several very valuable acquaintances, she said, at the Independent Chapel; and among others, lighted upon her friend of the Rookery, Mr. Grimes Wapshot. We did not know then the interview which he had had with Mr. Smithers, not did Grimes think proper to acquaint us with the particulars of it; but though I did acquaint Mrs. H. with the fact that her favourite preacher had been tried for forgery, *she* replied that she considered the story an atrocious calumny; and *he* answered by saying that Mary and I were in lamentable darkness, and that we should infallibly find the way to a certain bottomless pit, of which he seemed to know a great deal. Under the reverend gentleman's guidance and advice, she, after a time, separated from Saint Pancras altogether – '*sat under him*,' as the phrase is, regularly thrice a week – began to labour in the conversion of the poor of Bloomsbury and St. Giles's, and made a deal of baby-linen for distribution among those benighted people. She did not make any, however, for Mrs. Sam Titmarsh, who now showed signs that such would be speedily necessary, but let Mary (and my mother and sisters in Somersetshire) provide what was requisite for the coming event. I am not, indeed, sure that she did not say it was wrong on our parts to make any such provision, and that we ought to let the morrow provide for itself. At any rate, the Rev. Grimes Wapshot drank a deal of brandy-and-water at our house, and dined there even oftener than poor Gus used to do.

But I had little leisure to attend to him and his doings; for I must confess at this time I was growing very embarrassed in my circumstances, and was much harassed both as a private and public character.

As regards the former, Mrs. Hoggarty had given me 50*l*.; but out of that 50*l*. I had to pay a journey post from

Somersetshire, all the carriage of her goods from the country, the painting, papering, and carpeting of my house, the brandy and strong liquors drunk by the Rev. Grimes and his friends (for the reverend gent said that Rosolio did not agree with him); and finally, a thousand small bills and expenses incident to all housekeepers in the town of London.

Add to this, I received just at the time when I was most in want of cash, Madame Mantalini's bill, Messrs. Howell and James's ditto, the account of Baron von Stiltz, and the bill of Mr. Polonius for the setting of the diamond-pin. All these bills arrived in a week, as they have a knack of doing; and fancy my astonishment in presenting them to Mrs. Hoggarty, when she said, 'Well, my dear, you are in the receipt of a very fine income. If you choose to order dresses and jewels from first-rate shops, you must pay for them; and don't expect that *I* am to abet your extravagance, or give you a shilling more than the munificent sum I pay you for board and lodging!'

How could I tell Mary of this behaviour of Mrs. Hoggarty, and Mary in such a delicate condition! And bad as matters were at home I am sorry to say at the office they began to look still worse.

Not only did Roundhand leave, but Highmore went away. Abednego became head clerk: and one day old Abednego came to the place and was shown into the directors' private room; when he left it, he came trembling, chattering, and cursing downstairs; and had begun, 'Shentlemen –' a speech to the very clerks in the office, when Mr. Brough, with an imploring look, and crying out, 'Stop till Saturday!' at length got him into the street.

On Saturday Abednego, junior, left the office for ever, and I became head clerk with 400*l*. a year salary. It was a fatal week for the office, too. On Monday, when I arrived and took my seat at the head desk, and my first read of the newspaper, as was my right, the first thing I read was, 'Frightful fire in Houndsditch! Total destruction of Mr. Meshach's sealing-wax manufactory and of Mr. Shadrach's clothing depôt, adjoining. In the former was 20,000*l*. worth of the finest Dutch wax, which the voracious element attacked and devoured in a twinkling. The latter estimable gentleman had just completed 40,000 suits of clothes for the cavalry of H. H. the Cacique of Poyais.'

Both of these Jewish gents, who were connections of Mr. Abednego, were insured in our office to the full amount of their loss. The calamity was attributed to the drunkenness of a scoundrelly Irish watchman, who was employed on the premises, and who upset a bottle of whisky in the warehouse of Messrs. Shadrach, and incautiously looked for the liquor with a lighted candle. The man was brought to our office by his employers; and certainly, as we all could testify, was *even then* in a state of frightful intoxication.

As if this were not sufficient, in the obituary was announced the demise of Alderman Pash – Alderman Cally-Pash we used to call him in our lighter hours, knowing his propensity to green fat: but such a moment as this was no time for joking! He was insured by our house for 5,000*l*. And now I saw very well the truth of a remark of Gus's – viz. that life-insurance companies go on excellently for a year or two after their establishment, but that it is much more difficult to make them profitable when the assured parties begin to die.

The Jewish fires were the heaviest blows we had had; for though the Waddingley Cotton-mills had been burnt in 1822, at a loss to the company of 80,000*l*., and though the Patent Erostratus Match Manufactory had exploded in the same year at a charge of 14,000*l*., there were those who said that the loss had not been near so heavy as was supposed – nay, that the company had burnt the above-named establishments as adver-tisements for themselves. Of these facts I can't be positive, having never seen the early accounts of the concern.

Contrary to the expectation of all us gents, who were ourselves as dismal as mutes, Mr. Brough came to the office in his coach-and-four, laughing and joking with a friend as he stepped out of the door.

'Gentlemen!' said he, 'you have read the papers; they announce an event which I most deeply deplore. I mean the demise of the excellent Alderman Pash, one of our consti-tuents. But if anything can console me for the loss of that worthy man, it is to think that his children and widow will receive, at eleven o'clock next Saturday, 5,000*l*. from my friend Mr. Titmarsh, who is now head clerk here. As for the accident which has happened to Messrs. Shadrach and Meshach, – in *that*, at least, there is nothing that can occasion any person sorrow. On Saturday next, or as soon as the particulars of their loss can be satisfactorily ascertained, my friend Mr. Titmarsh will pay to them across the counter a sum of forty, fifty, eighty, one hundred thousand pounds – according to the amount of their loss. *They*, at least, will be remunerated; and though to our proprietors the outlay will no doubt be considerable, yet we can afford it, gentlemen. John Brough can afford it himself, for the matter of that, and not be very much embarrassed; and we must learn to bear ill-fortune as we have hitherto borne good, and show ourselves to be men always!'

Mr. B. concluded with some allusions, which I confess I don't like to give here; for to speak of heaven in connection with common wordly matters, has always appeared to me irreverent; and to bring it to bear witness to the lie in his mouth, as a religious hypocrite does, is such a frightful crime, that one should be careful even in alluding to it.

Mr. Brough's speech somehow found its way into the newspapers of that very evening; nor can I think who gave a report of it, for none of our gents left the office that day until the evening papers had appeared. But there was the speech – ay, and at the week's end, although Roundhand was heard on 'Change that day declaring he would bet five to one that Alderman Pash's money would never be paid, – at the week's end the money was paid by me to Mrs. Pash's solicitor across the counter, and no doubt Roundhand lost his money.

Shall I tell how the money was procured? There can be no harm in mentioning the matter now after twenty years' lapse of time; and moreover, it is greatly to the credit of two individuals now dead.

As I was head clerk, I had occasion to be frequently in Brough's room, and he now seemed once more disposed to take me into his confidence.

'Titmarsh my boy,' said he one day to me, after looking me hard in the face, 'did you ever hear of the fate of the great Mr. Silberschmidt, of London?' Of course I had. Mr. Silberschmidt, the Rothschild of his day (indeed I have heard the latter famous gent was originally a clerk in Silberschmidt's house) – Silberschmidt, fancying he could not meet his engagements, committed suicide; and had he lived till four o'clock that day, would have known that he was worth 400,000*l.* 'To tell you frankly the truth,' says Mr. B., 'I am in Silberschmidt's case. My late partner, Hoff, has given bills in the name of the firm to an enormous amount, and I have been obliged to meet them. I have been cast in fourteen actions, brought by creditors of that infernal Ginger Beer Company; and all the debts are put upon my shoulders, on account of my known wealth. Now, unless I have time, I cannot pay; and the long and short of the matter is that if I cannot procure, 5,000*l.* before Saturday, *our concern is ruined!*'

'What! the West Diddlesex ruined?' says I, thinking of my poor mother's annuity. 'Impossible! our business is splendid!'

'We must have 5,000*l.* on Saturday, and we are saved; and if you will, as you can, get it for me, I will give you 10,000*l.* for the money!'

B. then showed me to a fraction the accounts of the concern, and his own private account; proving beyond the possibility of a doubt, that with the 5,000*l.* our office must be set a-going; and without it that the concern must stop. No matter how he proved the thing; but there is, you know, a *dictum* of a statesman that, give him but leave to use figures, and he will prove anything.

I promised to ask Mrs. Hoggarty once more for the money, and she seemed not to be disinclined. I told him so; and that day he called upon her, his wife called upon her, his daughter called upon her, and once more the Brough carriage-and-four was seen at our house.

But Mrs. Brough was a bad manager; and instead of carrying matters with a high hand, fairly burst into tears before Mrs. Hoggarty, and went down on her knees and besought her to save dear John. This at once aroused my aunt's suspicions; and instead of lending the money she wrote off to Mr. Smithers instantly to come up to her, desired me to give her up the 3,000*l.* scrip shares that I possessed, called me an atrocious cheat and heartless, and vowed I had been the cause of her ruin.

How was Mr. Brough to get the money? I will tell you. Being in his room one day, old Gates the Fulham porter came and brought him from Mr. Balls, the pawnbroker, a sum of 1,200*l.* Missus told him he said, to carry the plate to Mr. Balls;

and having paid the money, old Gates fumbled a great deal in his pockets, and at last pulled out a 5*l*. note, which he said his daughter Jane had just sent him from service, and begged Mr. B. would let him have another share in the company. 'He was mortal sure it would go right yet. And when he heard master crying and cursing as he and missus were walking in the shrubbery, and saying that for the want of a few pounds – a few shillings – the finest fortune in Europe was to be overthrown, why Gates and his woman thought that they should come for'ard, to be sure, with all they could, to help the kindest master and missus ever was.'

This was the substance of Gates's speech; and Mr. Brough shook his hand and – took the 5*l*. 'Gates,' said he, 'that 5*l*. note shall be the best outlay you ever made in your life!' and I have no doubt it was, – but it was in heaven that poor old Gates was to get the interest of his little mite.

Nor was this the only instance. Mrs. Brough's sister, Miss Dough, who had been on bad terms with the director almost ever since he had risen to be a great man, came to the office with a power of attorney, and said, 'John, Isabella has been with me this morning, and says you want money, and I have brought you my 4,000*l*.; it is all I have, John, and pray God it may do you good – you and my dear sister, who was the best sister in the world to me till – till a little time ago.'

And she laid down the paper; I was called up to witness it, and Brough, with tears in his eyes, told me her words; for he could trust me, he said. And thus it was that I came to be present at Gates's interview with his master, which took place only an hour afterwards. Brave Mrs. Brough! how she was working for her husband! Good woman, and kind! but *you* had a true heart, and merited a better fate! Though wherefore say so? The woman, to this day, thinks her husband an angel, and loves him a thousand times better for his misfortunes.

On Saturday, Alderman Pash's solicitor was paid by me across the counter, as I said. 'Never mind your aunt's money, Titmarsh my boy,' said Brough: 'never mind her having resumed her shares; you are a true, honest fellow; you have never abused me like that pack of curs downstairs, and I'll make your fortune yet!'

The next week, as I was sitting with my wife, with Mr. Smithers, and with Mrs. Hoggarty, taking our tea comfortably, a knock was heard at the door, and a gentleman desired to speak to me in the parlour. It was Mr. Aminadab of Chancery Lane, who arrested me as a shareholder of the Independent West Diddlesex Association, at the suit of Von Stiltz of Clifford Street, Tailor and Draper.

I called down Smithers, and told him for heaven's sake not to tell Mary.

'Where is Brough?' says Mr. Smithers.

'Why,' says Mr. Aminadab, 'he's once more of the firm of Brough and Off, sir – he breakfasted at Calais this morning!'

CHAPTER XI

IN WHICH IT APPEARS THAT A MAN MAY POSSESS A DIAMOND AND YET BE VERY HARD PRESSED FOR A DINNER

On that fatal Saturday evening, in a hackney-coach, fetched from the Foundling, was I taken from my comfortable house and my dear little wife; whom Mr. Smithers was left to console as he might. He said that I was compelled to take a journey upon business connected with the office; and my poor Mary made up a little portmanteau of clothes, and tied a comforter round my neck, and bade my companion particularly to keep the coach-windows shut, which injunction the grinning wretch promised to obey. Our journey was not long; it was only a shilling fare to Cursitor Street, Chancery Lane, and there I was set down.

The house before which the coach stopped seemed to be only one of half-a-dozen in that street which were used for the same purpose. No man, be he ever so rich, can pass by those dismal houses, I think without a shudder. The front windows are barred, and on the dingy pillar of the door was a shining brass-plate, setting forth that 'Aminadab, Officer to the Sheriff of Middlesex,' lived therein. A little red-haired Israelite opened the first door as our coach drove up, and received me and my baggage.

As soon as we entered the door, he barred it, and I found myself in the face of another huge door, which was strongly locked; and, at last, passing through that, we entered the lobby of the house.

There is no need to describe it. It is very like ten thousand other houses in our dark city of London. There was a dirty passage and a dirty stair, and from the passage two dirty doors let into two filthy rooms, which had strong bars at the windows, and yet withal an air of horrible finery that makes

me uncomfortable to think of even yet. On the walls hung all
sorts of trumpery pictures in tawdry frames (how different
from those capital performances of my cousin Michael
Angelo!); on the mantelpiece huge French clocks, vases, and
candlesticks; on the sideboards, enormous trays of Birming-
ham plated-ware; for Mr. Aminadab not only arrested those
who could not pay money, but lent it to those who could; and
had already, in the way of trade, sold and bought these articles
many times over.

I agreed to take the back-parlour for the night, and while a
Hebrew damsel was arranging a little dusky sofa-bedstead
(woe betide him who has to sleep on it!) I was invited into the
front parlour, where Mr. Aminadab, bidding me to take
heart, told me I should have a dinner for nothing with a party
who had just arrived. I did not want for dinner, but I was glad
not to be alone – not alone, even till Gus came; for whom I
despatched a messenger to his lodgings hard by.

I found there, in the front parlour, at eight o'clock in the
evening, four gentleman, just about to sit down to dinner.
Surprising! there was Mr. B., a gentleman of fashion, who
had only within half-an-hour arrived in a post-chaise, with his
companion Mr. Lock, an officer of Horsham gaol. Mr. B.
was arrested in this wise: – He was a careless, good-humoured
gentleman, and had indorsed bills to a large amount for a
friend; who, a man of high family and unquestionable honour, had pledged the latter, along with a number of the most
solemn oaths, for the payment of the bills in question. Having
indorsed the notes, young Mr. B., with a proper thoughtless-
ness, forgot all about them, and so, by some chance, did the
friend whom he obliged; for, instead of being in London with
the money for the payment of his obligations, this latter
gentleman was travelling abroad, and never hinted one word
to Mr. B. that the notes would fall upon him. The young
gentleman was at Brighton lying sick of fever; was taken from
his bed by a bailiff, and carried, on a rainy day, to Horsham
gaol; had a relapse of his complaint, and when sufficiently
recovered, was brought up to London to the house of Mr.
Aminadab; where I found him – a pale, thin, good-humoured,
lost young man: he was lying on a sofa, and had given orders
for the dinner to which I was invited. The lad's face gave one

pain to look at; it was impossible not to see that his hours were numbered.

Now Mr. B. has not anything to do with my humble story; but I can't help mentioning him, as I saw him. He sent for his lawyer and his doctor; the former settled speedily his accounts with the bailiff, and the latter arranged all his earthly accounts: for after he went from the spunging-house he never recovered from the shock of the arrest, and in a few weeks he *died*. And though this circumstance took place many years ago, I can't forget it to my dying day; and often see the author of Mr. B.'s death, – a prosperous gentleman, riding a fine horse in the Park, lounging at the window of a club; with many friends, no doubt, and a good reputation. I wonder whether he has paid Mr. B.'s heirs the sum which that gentleman paid, and *died for*!

If Mr. B.'s history has nothing to do with mine, and is only inserted here for the sake of a moral, what business have I to mention particulars of the dinner to which I was treated by that gentleman, in the spunging-house in Cursitor Street? Why, for the moral too: and therefore the public must be told of what really and truly that dinner consisted.

There were five guests, and three silver tureens of soup: viz. mock-turtle soup, ox-tail soup, and giblet-soup. Next came a great piece of salmon, likewise on a silver dish, a roast goose, a roast saddle of mutton, roast game, and all sorts of adjuncts. In this way can a gentleman live in a spunging-house if he be inclined; and over this repast (which, in truth, I could not touch, for, let alone having dined, my heart was full of care) – over this meal my friend Gus Hoskins found me, when he received the letter that I had despatched to him.

Gus, who had never been in a prison before, and whose heart failed him as the red-headed young Moses opened and shut for him the numerous iron outer doors, was struck dumb to see me behind a bottle of claret, in a room blazing with gilt lamps; the curtains were down too, and you could not see the bars at the windows; and Mr. B., Mr. Lock the Brighton officer, Mr. Aminadab, and another rich gentleman of his trade and religious persuasion, were chirping as merrily, and looked as respectably, as any noblemen in the land.

'Have him in,' said Mr. B., 'if he's a friend of Mr. Titmarsh's; for, cuss me, I like to see a rogue: and run me through,

Titmarsh, but I think you are one of the best in London. You beat Brough; you do by Jove! for he looks like a rogue – anybody would swear to him: but you! by Jove you look the very picture of honesty!'

'A deep file,' said Aminadab, winking and pointing me out to his friend Mr. Jehoshaphat.

'A good one,' says Jehoshaphat.

'In for three hundred thousand pounds,' says Aminadab: 'Brough's right-hand man, and only three-and-twenty.'

'Mr. Titmarsh, sir, your 'ealth, sir,' says Mr. Lock, in an ecstasy of admiration. 'Your very good 'ealth, sir, and better luck to you next time.'

'Pooh, pooh! *he's* all right,' says Aminadab; 'let *him* alone.'

'In for *what*?' shouted I, quite amazed. 'Why, sir, you arrested me for 90*l*.'

'Yes, but you are in for half a million, – you know you are. *Them* debts I don't count – them paltry tradesmen's accounts. I mean Brough's business. It's an ugly one; but you'll get through it. We all know you; and I lay my life that when you come through the court, Mrs. Titmarsh has got a handsome thing laid by.'

'Mrs. Titmarsh has a small property, sir,' says I. 'What then?'

The three gentlemen burst into a loud laugh, said I was a 'rum chap' – a 'downy cove,' and made other remarks which I could not understand then; but the meaning of which I have since comprehended, for they took me to be a great rascal, I am sorry to say, and supposed that I had robbed the I. W. D. Association, and, in order to make my money secure, settled it on my wife.

It was in the midst of this conversation that, as I said, Gus came in; and whew! when he saw what was going on, he gave *such* a whistle!

'Herr von Joel, by Jove!' says Aminadab. At which all laughed.

'Sit down,' says Mr. B., – 'sit down, and whet your whistle, my piper! I say, egad! you're the piper that played before Moses! Had you there, Dab. Dab, get a fresh bottle of Burgundy for Mr. Hoskins.' And before he knew where he was, there was Gus for the first time in his life drinking Clot-

Vougeot. Gus said he had never tasted Bergamy before, at which the bailiff sneered, and told him the name of the wine.

'*Old Clo*! What?' says Gus; and we laughed: but the Hebrew gents did not this time.

'Come, come, sir!' says Mr. Aminadab's friend, 've're all shentlemen here, and shentlemen never makish reflexunsh upon other gentlemen'sh pershuashunsh.'

After this feast was concluded, Gus and I retired to my room to consult about my affairs. With regard to the responsibility incurred as a shareholder in the West Diddlesex, I was not uneasy; for though the matter might cause me a little trouble at first, I knew I was not a shareholder; that the shares were scrip shares, making the dividend payable to the bearer; and my aunt had called back her shares, and consequently I was free. But it was very unpleasant to me to consider that I was in debt nearly a hundred pounds to tradesmen, chiefly of Mrs. Hoggarty's recommendation; and as she had promised to be answerable for their bills, I determined to send her a letter reminding her of her promise, and begging her at the same time to relieve me from Mr. Von Stiltz's debt, for which I was arrested: and which was incurred not certainly at her desire, but at Mr. Brough's; and would never have been incurred by me but at the absolute demand of that gentleman.

I wrote to her, therefore, begging her to pay all these debts, and promised myself on Monday morning again to be with my dear wife. Gus carried off the letter, and promised to deliver it in Bernard Street after church time; taking care that Mary should know nothing at all of the painful situation in which I was placed. It was near midnight when we parted, and I tried to sleep as well as I could in the dirty little sofa-bedstead of Mr. Aminadab's back-parlour.

That morning was fine and sunshiny, and I heard all the bells ringing cheerfully for church, and longed to be walking to the Foundling with my wife: but there were the three iron doors between me and liberty, and I had nothing for it but to read my prayers in my own room, and walk up and down afterwards in the court at the back of the house. Would you believe it? This very court was like a cage! Great iron bars covered it in from one end to another; and here it was that Mr. Aminadab's gaol-birds took the air.

They had seen me reading out of the prayer-book at the back-parlour window, and all burst into a yell of laughter when I came to walk in the cage. One of them shouted out 'Amen!' when I appeared; another called me a muff (which means, in the slang language, a very silly fellow); a third wondered that I took to my prayer-book *yet*.

'When do you mean, sir?' says I to the fellow – a rough man, a horse-dealer.

'Why, when you are going *to be hanged*, you young hypocrite!' says the man. 'But that is always the way with Brough's people,' continued he. 'I had four greys once for him – a great bargain, but he would not go to look at them at Tattersall's, nor speak a word of business about them, because it was a Sunday.'

'Because there are hypocrites, sir,' says I, 'religion is not to be considered a bad thing; and if Mr. Brough would not deal with you on a Sunday, he certainly did his duty.'

The men only laughed the more at this rebuke, and evidently considered me a great criminal. I was glad to be released from their society by the appearance of Gus and Mr. Smithers. Both wore very long faces. They were ushered into my room, and, without any orders of mine, a bottle of wine and biscuits were brought in by Mr. Aminadab; which I really thought was very kind of him.

'Drink a glass of wine, Mr. Titmarsh,' says Smithers,' and read this letter. A pretty note was that which you sent to your aunt this morning, and here you have an answer to it.'

I drank the wine, and trembled rather as I read as follows:-

'SIR, –

'If, because you knew I had desined to leave you my proparty, you wished to murdar me, and so stepp into it, you are dissapointed. Your *villiany* and *ingratatude would* have murdard me, had I not, by Heaven's grace, been inabled to look for consalation *elsewhere*.

'For nearly a year I have been a *martar* to you. I gave up everything, – my happy home in the country, where all respected the name of Hoggarty; my valuble furnitur and wines; my plate, glass, and crockry; I brought all – all to make your home happy and rispectable. I put up with the *airs and impertanencies* of Mrs. Titmarsh; I loaded her and you with presents and bennafits. I sacrafised myself; I gave up the best sociaty in the land, to witch I have been accustomed, in order to be a guardian and compannion to you, and prevent, if possible, that *waist and ixtravygance* which I *prophycied* would be your ruin. Such waist and ixtravygance never, never, never did I see. Buttar waisted as if it had been dirt, coles flung away, candles burnt *at both ends*, tea and meat the same. The butcher's bill in this house was enough to support six famalies.

'And now you have the audassaty, being placed in prison justly for your crimes, – for cheating me of 3,000*l.*, for robbing your mother of an insignificient summ, which to her, poor thing, was everything (though she will not feel her loss as I do, being all her life next door to a beggar), for incurring detts which you cannot pay, wherein you knew that your miserable income was quite unable to support your ixtravygance – you come upon me to pay your detts! No, sir, it is quite enough that your mother should go on the parish, and that your wife should sweep the streets, to which you have indeed brought them; *I*, at least, though cheated by you of a large summ, and obliged to pass my days in comparitive ruin, can retire, and have some of the comforts to which my rank entitles me. The furnitur in this house is mine; and as I presume you intend *your lady* to sleep in the streets, I give you warning that I shall remove it all to-morrow.

'Mr. Smithers will tell you that I had intended to leave you my intire fortune. I have this morning, in his presents, solamly toar up my will; and hereby renounce all connection with you and your beggarly family.

'SUSAN HOGGARTY.

'P.S. – I took a viper into my bosom, *and it stung me.*'
I confess that, on the first reading of this letter, I was in such a fury that I forgot almost the painful situation in which it plunged me, and the ruin hanging over me.

'What a fool you were, Titmarsh, to write that letter,' said Mr. Smithers. 'You have cut your own throat, sir, – lost a fine property, – written yourself out of five hundred a year. Mrs.

Hoggarty, my client, brought the will, as she says, down-stairs, and flung it into the fire before our faces.'

'It's a blessing that your wife was from home,' added Gus. 'She went to church this morning with Dr. Salts' family, and sent word that she would spend the day with them. She was always glad to be away from Mrs. H., you know.'

'She never knew on which side her bread was buttered,' said Mr. Smithers. 'You should have taken the lady when she was in the humour, sir, and have borrowed the money elsewhere. Why, sir, I had almost reconciled her to her loss in that cursed company. I showed her how I had saved out of Brough's claws the whole of her remaining fortune; which he would have devoured in a day, the scoundrel! And if you would have left the matter to me, Mr. Titmarsh, I would have had you reconciled completely to Mrs. Hoggarty; I would have removed all your difficulties; I would have lent you the pitiful sum of money myself.'

'Will you?' says Gus; 'that's a trump!' and he seized Smithers's hand, and squeezed it so that the tears came into the attorney's eyes.

'Generous fellow!' said I; 'lend me money, when you know what a situation I am in, and not able to pay!'

'Ay, my good sir, there's the rub!' says Mr. Smithers. 'I said I *would* have lent the money; and so to the acknowledged heir of Mrs. Hoggarty I would – would at this moment; for nothing delights the heart of Bob Smithers more than to do a kindness. I would have rejoiced in doing it; and a mere acknowledgment from that respected lady would have amply sufficed. But now, sir, the case is altered, – you have no security to offer, as you justly observe.'

'Not a whit, certainly,'

'And without security, sir, of course can expect no money – of course not. You are a man of the world, Mr. Titmarsh, and I see our notions exactly agree.'

'There's his wife's property,' says Gus.

'Wife's property? Bah! Mrs. Sam Titmarsh is a minor, and can't touch a shilling of it. No, no, no meddling with minors for me! But stop! – your mother has a house and shop in our village. Get me a mortgage of that – '

'I'll do no such thing, sir,' says I. 'My mother has suffered quite enough on my score already and has my sisters to provide for; and I will thank you, Mr. Smithers, not to breathe a syllable to her regarding my present situation.'

'You speak like a man of honour, sir,' says Mr. Smithers, 'and I will obey your injunctions to the letter. I will do more, sir. I will introduce you to a respectable firm here, my worthy friends, Messrs. Higgs, Biggs, and Blatherwick, who will do everything in their power to serve you. And so, sir, I wish you a very good morning.'

And with this Mr. Smithers took his hat and left the room; and after a further consultation with my aunt, as I heard afterwards, quitted London that evening by the mail.

I sent my faithful Gus off once more to break the matter gently to my wife, fearing lest Mrs. Hoggarty should speak of it abruptly to her; as I knew in her anger she would do. But he came in an hour panting back, to say that Mrs. H. had packed and locked her trunks, and had gone off in a hackney-coach. So knowing that my poor Mary was not to return till night, Hoskins remained with me till then; and after a dismal day, left me once more at nine, to carry the dismal tidings to her.

At ten o'clock on that night there was a great rattling and ringing at the outer door, and presently my poor girl fell into my arms; and Gus Hoskins sat blubbering in a corner as I tried my best to console her.

The next morning I was favoured with a visit from Mr. Blatherwick; who, hearing from me that I had only three guineas in my pocket, told me very plainly that lawyers only lived by fees. He recommended me to quit Cursitor Street, as living there was very expensive. And as I was sitting very sad, my wife made her appearance (it was with great difficulty that she could be brought to leave me the night previous), –

'The horrible men came at four this morning,' said she; 'four hours before light.'

'What horrible men?' says I.

'Your aunt's men,' said she, 'to remove the furniture; they had it all packed before I came away. And I let them carry all,' said she: 'I was too sad to look what was ours and what was not. That odious Mr. Wapshot was with them; and I left him seeing the last waggon-load from the door. I have only brought away your clothes,' added she, 'and a few of mine; and some of the books you used to like to read; and some – some things I have been getting for the – for the baby. The servants' wages were paid up to Christmas; and I paid them the rest. And see! just as I was going away, the post came and brought to me my half-year's income – 35*l*., dear Sam. Isn't it a blessing?'

'Will you pay my bill, Mr. What-d'ye-call'im!' here cried Mr. Aminadab, flinging open the door (he had been consulting with Mr. Blatherwick, I suppose). 'I want the room for *a gentleman*. I guess it's too dear for the like of you.' And here – will you believe it? – the man handed me a bill of three guineas for two days' board and lodging in his odious house.

There was a crowd of idlers round the door as I passed out of it, and had I been alone I should have been ashamed of seeing them; but, as it was, I was only thinking of my dear, dear wife, who was leaning trustfully on my arm, and smiling like heaven into my face – ay, and *took* heaven, too, into the Fleet prison with me – or an angel out of heaven. Ah! I had loved her before, and happy it is to love when one is hopeful and young in the midst of smiles and sunshine; but be *un*happy, and then see what it is to be loved by a good woman! I declare before heaven, that of all the joys and happy moments it has given me, that was the crowning one – that little ride, with my wife's cheek on my shoulder, down Holborn to the prison! Do you think I cared for the bailiff that sat opposite? No, by the Lord! I kissed her, and hugged her – yes, and cried with her likewise. But before our ride was over her eyes dried up, and she stepped blushing and happy out of the coach at the prison-door, as if she were a princess going to the Queen's drawing-room.

CHAPTER XII

IN WHICH THE HERO'S DIAMOND MAKES ACQUAINTANCE WITH THE HERO'S UNCLE

The failure of the great Diddlesex Association speedily became the theme of all the newspapers, and every person concerned in it was soon held up to public abhorrence as a rascal and a swindler. It was hinted that poor I had sent a hundred thousand pounds to America, and only waited to pass through the court in order to be a rich man for the rest of my days. This opinion had some supporters in the prison; where, strange to say, it procured me consideration – of which, as may be supposed, I was little inclined to avail myself. Mr. Aminadab, however, in his frequent visits to the Fleet, persisted in saying that I was a poor-spirited creature, a mere tool in Brough's hands, and had not saved a shilling. Opinions, however, differed; and I believe it was considered by the turnkeys that I was a fellow of exquisite dissimulation, who had put on the appearance of poverty in order more effectually to mislead the public.

Messrs. Abednego and Son were similarly held up to public odium: and, in fact, what were the exact dealings of these gentlemen with Mr. Brough I have never been able to learn. It was proved by the books that large sums of money had been paid to Mr. Abednego by the Company; but he produced documents signed by Mr. Brough, which made the latter and the West Diddlesex Association his debtors to a still further amount. On the day I went to the Bankruptcy Court to be examined, Mr. Abednego and the two gentlemen from Houndsditch were present to swear to their debts, and made a sad noise, and uttered a vast number of oaths in attestation of their claim. But Messrs. Jackson and Paxton produced against them that very Irish porter who was said to have been the cause of the fire, and, I am told, hinted that they had matter for hanging the Jewish gents if they persisted in their demand. On this they disappeared altogether, and no more was ever heard of their losses. I am inclined to believe that our director had had money from Abednego – had given him shares as bonus and security – had been suddenly obliged to redeem these shares with ready money; and so had precipitated the ruin of himself and the concern. It is needless to say here in what a multiplicity of companies Brough was engaged. That in which poor Mr. Tidd invested his money, did not pay 2*d*. in the pound; and that was the largest dividend paid by any of them.

As for ours – ah! there was a pretty scene as I was brought from the Fleet to the Bankruptcy Court, to give my testimony as late head clerk and accountant of the West Diddlesex Association.

My poor wife, then very near her time, insisted upon accompanying me to Basinghall Street; and so did my friend Gus Hoskins, that true and honest fellow. If you had seen the crowd that was assembled, and the hubbub that was made as I was brought up!

'Mr. Titmarsh,' says the Commission as I came to the table, with a peculiar sarcastic accent on the Tit – 'Mr. Titmarsh, you were the confidant of Mr. Brough, the principal clerk of Mr. Brough, and a considerable shareholder in the company?'

'Only a nominal one, sir,' said I.

'Of course, only nominal,' continued the Commissioner, turning to his colleague with a sneer; 'and a great comfort it must be to you, sir, to think that you had a share in all the plun – the profits of the speculation, and now can free yourself from the losses, by saying you are only a nominal sharehol-der.'

'The infernal villain!' shouted out a voice from the crowd. It was that of the furious half-pay captain and late shareholder, Captain Sparr.

'Silence in the court there!' the Commission continued: and all this while Mary was anxiously looking in his face, and then in mine, as pale as death; while Gus, on the contrary, was as red as vermilion. 'Mr. Titmarsh, I have had the good fortune to see a list of your debts from the Insolvent Court, and find that you are indebted to Mr. Stiltz, the great tailor, in a handsome sum; to Mr. Polonius, the celebrated jeweller, likewise; to fashionable milliners and dress-makers, moreover; – and all this upon a salary of 200*l*. per annum. For so young a gentleman, it must be confessed you have employed your time well.'

'Has this anything to do with the question, sir?' says I. 'Am I here to give an account of my private debts, or to speak as to what I know regarding the affairs of the company? As for my share in it, I have a mother, sir, and many sisters – '

'The d—d scoundrel!' shouts the captain.

'Silence that there fellow!' shouts Gus, as bold as brass; at which the court burst out laughing, and this gave me courage to proceed.

'My mother, sir, four years since, having a legacy of 400*l*. left to her, advised with her solicitor, Mr. Smithers, how she should dispose of this sum; and as the Independent West Diddlesex was just then established, the money was placed in an annuity in that office, where I procured a clerkship. You may suppose me a very hardened criminal, because I have ordered clothes of Mr. Von Stiltz; but you will hardly fancy that I, a lad of nineteen, knew anything of the concerns of the company into whose service I entered as twentieth clerk, my own mother's money paying, as it were, for my place. Well, sir, the interest offered by the company was so tempting, that a rich relative of mine was induced to purchase a number of shares.'

'*Who* induced your relative, if I may make so bold as to inquire?'

'I can't help owning, sir,' says I, blushing, 'that I wrote a letter myself. But consider, my relative was sixty years old, and I was twenty-one. My relative took several months to consider, and had the advice of her lawyers before she acceded to my request. And I made it at the instigation of Mr. Brough, who dictated the letter which I wrote, and who I really thought then was as rich as Mr. Rothschild himself.'

'Your friend placed her money in your name; and you, if I mistake not, Mr. Titmarsh, were suddenly placed over the heads of twelve of your fellow-clerks as a reward for your service in obtaining it?'

'It is very true, sir,' – and, as I confessed it, poor Mary began to wipe her eyes, and Gus's ears (I could not see his face) looked like two red-hot muffins – 'it's quite true, sir; and, as matters have turned out, I am heartily sorry for what I did. But at the time I thought I could serve my aunt as well as myself; and you must remember, then, how high our shares were.'

'Well, sir, having procured this sum of money, you were straightway taken into Mr. Brough's confidence. You were received into his house, and from third clerk speedily became head clerk; in which post you were found at the disappearance of your worthy patron!'

'Sir, you have no right to question me, to be sure; but here are a hundred of our shareholders, and I'm not unwilling to make a clean breast of it,' said I, pressing Mary's hand. 'I certainly *was* the head clerk. And why? Because the other gents left the office. I certainly was received into Mr. Brough's house. And why? Because, sir, *my aunt had more money to lay out*. I see it all clearly now, though I could not understand it then; and the proof that Mr. Brough wanted my aunt's money, and not me, is that, when she came to town, our director carried her by force out of my house to Fulham, and never so much as thought of asking me or my wife thither. Ay, sir, and he would have had her remaining money, had not her lawyer from the country prevented her disposing of it. Before the concern finally broke, and as soon as she heard there was doubt concerning it, she took back her shares – scrip shares they were, sir, as you know – and has disposed of them as she thought fit. Here, sir, and gents,' says I 'you have the whole of the history as far as regards me. In order to get her only son a means of livelihood, my mother placed her little money with the company – it is lost. My aunt invested larger sums with it, which were to have been mine one day, and they are lost too; and here am I, at the end of four years, a disgraced and ruined man. Is there any one present, however much he has suffered by the failure of the company, that has had worse fortune through it than I?'

'Mr. Titmarsh,' says Mr. Commissioner, in a much more friendly way, and at the same time casting a glance at a newspaper reporter that was sitting hard by, 'your story is not likely to get into the newspapers; for, as you say, it is a private affair, which you had no need to speak of unless you thought proper, and may be considered as a confidential conversation between us and the other gentlemen here. But if it *could* be made public, it might do some good, and warn people, if they *will* be warned, against the folly of such enterprises as that in which you have been engaged. It is quite clear from your story, that you have been deceived as grossly as any one of the persons present. But look you, sir, if you had not been so eager after gain, I think you would not have allowed yourself to be deceived, and would have kept your relative's money, and inherited it, accordingly to your story, one day or other. Directly people expect to make a large interest, their judgment seems to desert them; and because they wish for profit, they think they are sure of it, and disregard all warnings and all prudence. Besides the hundreds of honest families who have been ruined by merely placing confidence in this Association of yours, and who deserve the heartiest pity, there are hundreds more who have embarked in it, like yourself, not for investment, but for speculation; and these, upon my word, deserve the fate they have met with. As long as dividends are paid, no questions are asked; and Mr. Brough might have taken the money for his shareholders on the high road, and they would have pocketed it, and not been too curious. But what's the use of talking?' says Mr. Commissioner, in a passion: 'here is one rogue detected, and a thousand dupes made; and if another swindler starts tomorrow, there will be a thousand more of his victims round this table a year hence; and so, I suppose, to the end. And now let's go to business, gentlemen, and excuse this sermon.'

After giving an account of all I knew, which was very little, other gents who were employed in the concern were examined; and I went back to prison, with the poor little wife on my arm. We had to pass through the crowd in the rooms, and my heart bled as I saw, amongst a score of others, poor Gates, Brough's porter, who had advanced every shilling to his master, and was now, with ten children, houseless and penniless in his old age. Captain Sparr was in this neighbourhood, but by no means so friendly disposed; for while Gates touched his hat, as if I had been a lord, the little captain came forward threatening with his bamboo-cane, and swearing with great oaths that I was an accomplice of Brough. 'Curse you for a smooth-faced scoundrel!' says he. 'What business have you to ruin an English gentleman, as you have me?' And again he advanced with his stick. But this time, officer as he was, Gus took him by the collar, and shoved him back, and said, 'Look at the lady, you brute, and hold your tongue!' And when he looked at my wife's situation, Captain Sparr became redder for shame than he had before been for anger. 'I'm sorry she's married to such a good-for-nothing,' muttered he, and fell back; and my poor wife and I walked out of the court, and back to our dismal room in the prison.

It was a hard place for a gentle creature like her to be confined in; and I longed to have some of my relatives with her when her time should come. But her grandmother could not leave the old lieutenant; and my mother had written to say that, as Mrs. Hoggarty was with us, she was quite as well at home with her children. 'What a blessing it is for you, under your misfortunes,' continued the good soul, 'to have the generous purse of your aunt for succour!' Generous purse of my aunt, indeed! Where could Mrs. Hoggarty be? It was evident that she had not written to any of her friends in the country, nor gone thither, as she threatened.

But as my mother had already lost so much money through my unfortunate luck, and as she had enough to do with her little pittance to keep my sisters at home; and as, on hearing of my condition, she would infallibly have sold her last gown to bring me aid, Mary and I agreed that we would not let her know what our real condition was – bad enough! heaven knows, and sad and cheerless. Old Lieutenant Smith had likewise nothing but his half-pay and his rheumatism; so we were, in fact, quite friendless.

That period of my life, and that horrible prison, seem to me like recollections of some fever. What an awful place! – not for the sadness, strangely enough, as I thought, but for the gaiety of it; for the long prison galleries were, I remember, full of life and a sort of grave bustle. All day and all night doors were clapping to and fro; and you heard loud voices, oaths, footsteps, and laughter. Next door to our room was one where a man sold gin, under the name of *tape*; and here, from morning till night, the people kept up a horrible revelry; and sang – sad songs some of them: but my dear little girl was, thank God! unable to understand the most part of their ribaldry. She never used to go out till nightfall; and all day she sat working at a little store of caps and dresses for the expected stranger – and not, she says to this day, unhappy. But the confinement sickened her, who had been used to happy country air, and she grew daily paler and paler.

The Fives' Court was opposite our window; and here I used, very unwillingly at first, but afterwards, I do confess, with much eagerness, to take a couple of hours' daily sport. Ah! it was a strange place. There was an aristocracy there as elsewhere, – amongst other gents, a son of my Lord Deuceace; and many of the men in the prison were as eager to walk with him, and talked of his family as knowingly, as if they were Bond Street bucks. Poor Tidd, especially, was one of these. Of all his fortune he had nothing left but a dressing-case and a flowered dressing-gown; and to these possessions he added a fine pair of moustaches, with which the poor creature strutted about; and though cursing his ill-fortune, was, I do believe, as happy whenever his friends brought him a guinea, as he had been during his brief career as a gentleman on town. I have seen sauntering dandies in watering-places ogling the women, watching eagerly for steamboats and stage-coaches as if their lives depended upon them, and strutting all day in jackets up and down the public walks. Well, there are such fellows in prisons; quite as dandified and foolish, only a little more shabby – dandies with dirty beards and holes at their elbows.

I did not go near what is called the poor side of the prison – I *dared* not, that was the fact. But our little stock of money was running low; and my heart sickened to think what might be my dear wife's fate, and on what sort of a couch our child might be born. But heaven spared me that pang – heaven, and my dear, good friend, Gus Hoskins.

The attorneys to whom Mr. Smithers recommended me, told me that I could get leave to live in the rules of the Fleet, could I procure sureties to the marshal of the prison for the amount of the detainer lodged against me; but though I looked Mr. Blatherwick hard in the face, he never offered to give the bail for me, and I knew no housekeeper in London who would procure it. There was, however, one whom I did not know, – and that was old Mr. Hoskins, the leatherseller of Skinner Street, a kind, fat gentleman, who brought his fat wife to see Mrs. Titmarsh; and though the lady gave herself rather patronizing airs (her husband being free of the Skinners' Company, and bidding fair to be Alderman, nay, Lord Mayor of the first city in the world), she seemed heartily to sympathize with us: and her husband stirred and bustled about until the requisite leave was obtained, and I was allowed comparative liberty.

As for lodgings, they were soon had. My old landlady, Mrs. Stokes, sent her Jemima to say that her first floor was at our service; and when we had taken possession of it, and I offered at the end of the week to pay her bill, the good soul, with tears in her eyes, told me that she did not want for money now, and that she knew I had enough to do with what I had. I did not refuse her kindess; for, indeed, I had but five guineas left, and ought not by rights to have thought of such expensive apartments as hers: but my wife's time was very near, and I could not bear to think that she should want for any comfort in her lying-in.

That admirable woman, with whom the Misses Hoskins came every day to keep company – and very nice, kind ladies they are – recovered her health a good deal, now she was out of the odious prison and was enabled to take exercise. How gaily did we pace up and down Bridge Street and Chatham Place, to be sure! and yet, in truth, I was a beggar, and felt sometimes ashamed of being so happy.

With regard to the liabilities of the Company my mind was now made quite easy; for the creditors could only come upon our directors, and these it was rather difficult to find. Mr. Brough was across the water; and I must say, to the credit of that gentleman, that while everybody thought he had run away with hundreds of thousands of pounds, he was in a garret at Boulogne, with scarce a shilling in his pocket, and his fortune to make afresh. Mrs. Brough, like a good, brave woman, remained faithful to him, and only left Fulham with the gown on her back; and Miss Belinda, though grumbling and sadly out of temper, was no better off. For the other

directors, – when they came to inquire at Edinburgh for Mr.
Mull, W.D., it appeared there *was* a gentleman of that name,
who had practised in Edinburgh, with good reputation until
1800, since when he had retired to the Isle of Skye; and on
being applied to, knew no more of the West Diddlesex
Association than Queen Anne did. General Sir Dionysius
O'Halloran had abruptly quitted Dublin, and returned to the
republic of Guatemala. Mr. Shirk went into the *Gazette*. Mr.
Macraw, M.P., and King's counsel, had not a single guinea in
the world but what he received for attending our board; and
the only man seizable was Mr. Manstraw, a wealthy navy
contractor, as we understood, at Chatham. He turned out to
be a small dealer in marine stores, and his whole stock in trade
was not worth 10*l*. Mr. Abednego was the other director, and
we have already seen what became of *him*.

'Why, as there is no danger from the West Diddlesex,'
suggested Mr. Hoskins, senior, 'should you not now
endeavour to make an arrangement with your creditors; and
who can make a better bargain with them than pretty Mrs.
Titmarsh here, whose sweet eyes would soften the hardest-
hearted tailor or milliner that ever lived?'

Accordingly, my dear girl, one bright day in February,
shook me by the hand, and bidding me be of good cheer, set
off with Gus in a coach, to pay a visit to those persons. Little
did I think a year before, that the daughter of the gallant Smith
should ever be compelled to be a suppliant to tailors and
haberdashers; but *she*, heaven bless her! felt none of the shame
which oppressed me – or *said* she felt none – and went away,
nothing doubting, on her errand.

In the evening she came back, and my heart thumped to
know the news. I saw it was bad by her face. For some time
she did not speak, but looked as pale as death, and wept as she
kissed me. '*You* speak, Mr. Augustus,' at last said she,
sobbing; and so Gus told me the circumstances of that dismal
day.

'What do you think, Sam?' says he; 'that infernal aunt of
yours, at whose command you had the things, has written to
the tradesmen to say that you are a swindler and impostor;
that you give out that *she* ordered the goods; that she is ready
to drop down dead, and to take her bible-oath she never did

any such thing, and that they must look to you alone for payment. Not one of them would hear of letting you out; and as for Mantalini, the scoundrel was so insolent that I gave him a box on the ear, and would have half-killed him, only poor Mary – Mrs. Titmarsh I mean – screamed and fainted: and I brought her away, and here she is, as ill as can be.'

That night the indefatigable Gus was obliged to run post-haste for Doctor Salts, and next morning a little boy was born. I did not know whether to be sad or happy, as they showed me the little weakly thing; but Mary was the happiest woman, she declared, in the world, and forgot all her sorrows in nursing the poor baby: she went bravely through her time, and vowed that it was the loveliest child in the world; and that though Lady Tiptoff, whose confinement we read of as having taken place the same day, might have a silk bed and a fine house in Grosvenor Square, she never, never could have such a beautiful child as our dear little Gus; for after whom should we have named the boy, if not after our good, kind friend? We had a little party at the christening, and I assure you were very merry over our tea.

The mother, thank heaven! was very well, and it did one's heart good to see her in that attitude in which I think every woman, be she ever so plain, looks beautiful – with her baby at her bosom. The child was sickly, but she did not see it; we were very poor, but what cared she? She had no leisure to be sorrowful as I was; I had my last guinea now in my pocket; and when *that* was gone – ah! my heart sickened to think of what was to come, and I prayed for strength and guidance, and in the midst of my perplexities felt yet thankful that the danger of the confinement was over; and that for the worse fortune which was to befall us, my dear wife was at least prepared, and strong in health.

I told Mrs. Stokes that she must let us have a cheaper room – a garret that should cost but a few shillings; and though the good woman bade me remain in the apartments we occupied, yet, now that my wife was well, I felt it would be a crime to deprive my kind landlady of her chief means of livelihood; and at length she promised to get me a garret as I wanted, and to make it as comfortable as might be; and little

Jemima declared that she would be glad beyond measure to wait on the mother and the child.

The room, then, was made ready; and though I took some pains not to speak of the arrangement too suddenly to Mary, yet there was no need of disguise or hesitation; for when at last I told her – 'Is that all?' said she, and took my hand with one of her blessed smiles, and vowed that she and Jemima would keep the room as pretty and neat as possible. 'And I will cook your dinners,' added she; 'for you know you said I make the best roly-poly puddings in the world.' God bless her! I do think some women almost love poverty: but I did not tell Mary how poor I was, nor had she any idea how lawyers', and prisons', and doctors' fees had diminished the sum of money which she brought me when we came to the Fleet.

It was not, however, destined that she and her child should inhabit that little garret. We were to leave our lodgings on Monday morning; but on Saturday evening the child was seized with convulsions, and all Sunday the mother watched and prayed for it: but it pleased God to take the innocent infant from us, and on Sunday, at midnight, it lay a corpse in its mother's bosom. Amen. We have other children, happy and well, now round about us, and from the father's heart the memory of this little thing has almost faded; but I do believe that every day of her life the mother thinks of the firstborn that was with her for so short a while: many and many a time has she taken her daughters to the grave, in Saint Bride's, where he lies buried; and she wears still at her neck a little, little lock of gold hair, which she took from the head of the infant as he lay smiling in his coffin. It has happened to me to forget the child's birth-day, but to her never; and often, in the midst of common talk, comes something that shows she is thinking of the child still, – some simple allusion that is to me inexpressibly affecting.

I shall not try to describe her grief, for such things are sacred and secret; and a man has no business to place them on paper for all the world to read. Nor should I have mentioned the child's loss at all, but that even that loss was the means of a great worldly blessing to us; as my wife has often with tears and thanks acknowledged.

While my wife was weeping over her child, I am ashamed to say I was distracted with other feelings besides those of grief for its loss; and I have often since thought what a master – nay, destroyer – of the affections want is, and have learned from experience to be thankful for *daily bread*. That acknowledgment of weakness which we make in imploring to be relieved from hunger and from temptation, is surely wisely put in our daily prayer. Think of it you who are rich, and take heed how you turn a beggar away.

The child lay there in its wicker cradle, with its sweet fixed smile in its face (I think the angels in heaven must have been glad to welcome that pretty innocent smile); and it was only the next day, after my wife had gone to lie down, and I sat keeping watch by it, that I remembered the condition of its parents, and thought, I can't tell with what a pang, that I had not money left to bury the little thing, and wept bitter tears of despair. Now, at last, I thought I must apply to my poor mother, for this was a sacred necessity; and I took paper, and wrote her a letter at the baby's side, and told her of our condition. But, thank heaven! I never sent the letter; for as I went to the desk to get sealing-wax and seal that dismal letter, my eyes fell upon the diamond-pin that I had quite forgotten, and that was lying in the drawer of the desk.

I looked into the bedroom, – my poor wife was asleep; she had been watching for three nights and days, and had fallen asleep from sheer fatigue; and I ran out to a pawnbroker's with the diamond, and received seven guineas for it, and coming back put the money into the landlady's hand, and told her to get what was needful. My wife was still asleep when I came back; and when she woke, we persuaded her to go downstairs to the landlady's parlour; and meanwhile the necessary preparations were made, and the poor child consigned to its coffin.

The next day, after all was over, Mrs. Stokes gave me back three out of the seven guineas; and then I could not help sobbing out to her my doubts and wretchedness, telling her that this was the last money I had; and when that was gone, I knew not what was to become of the best wife that ever a man was blest with.

My wife was downstairs with the woman. Poor Gus, who was with me, and quite as much affected as any of the party, took me by the arm, and led me downstairs; and we quite forgot all about the prison and the rules, and walked a long, long way across Blackfriars Bridge, the kind fellow striving as much as possible to console me.

When we came back, it was in the evening. The first person who met me in the house was my kind mother, who fell into my arms with many tears, and who rebuked me tenderly for not having told her of my necessities. She never should have known of them, she said; but she had not heard from me since I wrote announcing the birth of the child, and she felt uneasy about my silence; and meeting Mr. Smithers in the street asked from him news concerning me: whereupon that gentleman with some little show of alarm, told her that he thought her daughter-in-law was confined in an uncomfortable place; that Mrs. Hoggarty had left us; finally, that I was in prison. This news at once despatched my poor mother on her travels, and she had only just come from the prison, where she learned my address.

I asked her whether she had seen my wife, and how she found her. Rather to my amaze she said that Mary was out with the landlady when she arrived; and eight – nine o'clock came, and she was absent still.

At ten o'clock returned – not my wife, but Mrs. Stokes, and with her a gentleman, who shook hands with me on coming into the room and said, 'Mr. Titmarsh, I don't know whether you will remember me: my name is Tiptoff. I have brought you a note from Mrs. Titmarsh, and a message from my wife, who sincerely commiserates your loss, and begs you will not be uneasy at Mrs. Titmarsh's absence. She has been good enough to promise to pass the night with Lady Tiptoff; and I am sure you will not object to her being away from you, while she is giving happiness to a sick mother and a sick child.' After a few more words, my lord left us. My wife's note only said that Mrs. Stokes would tell me all.

CHAPTER XIII

IN WHICH IT IS SHOWN THAT A GOOD WIFE IS THE BEST DIAMOND A MAN CAN WEAR IN HIS BOSOM

'Mrs. Titmarsh, ma'am,' says Mrs. Stokes, 'before I gratify your curiosity, ma'am, permit me to observe that angels is scarce; and it's rare to have one, much more two, in a family. Both your son and your daughter-in-law, ma'am, are of that uncommon sort; they are, now, reely, ma'am.'

My mother said she thanked God for both of us; and Mrs. Stokes proceeded:-

'When the fu— when the seminary, ma'am, was concluded this morning, your poor daughter-in-law was glad to take shelter in my humble parlour, ma'am; where she wept, and told a thousand stories of the little cherub that's gone. Heaven bless us! it was here but a month, and no one could have thought it could have done such a many things in that time. But a mother's eyes are clear, ma'am; and I had just such another angel, my dear little Antony, that was born before Jemima, and would have been twenty-three now were he in this wicked world, ma'am. However, I won't speak of him, ma'am, but of what took place.

'You must know, ma'am, that Mrs. Titmarsh remained downstairs while Mr. Samuel was talking with his friend Mr. Hoskins; and the poor thing would not touch a bit of dinner, though we had it made comfortable; and after dinner, it was with difficulty I could get her to sup a little drop of wine-and-water, and dip a toast in it. It was the first morsel that had passed her lips for many a long hour, ma'am.

'Well, she would not speak, and I thought it best not to interrupt her; but she sat and looked at my two youngest that were playing on the rug; and just as Mr. Titmarsh, and his friend Gus went out, the boy brought the newspaper, ma'am,

– it always comes from three to four, and I began a-reading of it. But I couldn't read much, for thinking of poor Mr. Sam's sad face as he went out, and the sad story he told me about his money being so low; and every now and then I stopped reading, and bade Mrs. T. not to take on so; and told her some stories about my dear little Antony.

'"Ah!" says she, sobbing, and looking at the young ones, "you have other children, Mrs. Stokes; but that – that was my only one;" and she flung back in her chair, and cried fit to break her heart: and I knew that the cry would do her good, and so went back to my paper – the *Morning Post*, ma'am; I always read it, for I like to know what's a-going on in the West End.

'The very first thing that my eyes lighted upon was this: – "Wanted, immediately, a respectable person as wet-nurse. Apply at No. — , Grosvenor Square." "Bless us and save us!" says I, "here's poor Lady Tiptoff ill;" for I knew her ladyship's address, and how she was confined on the very same day with Mrs. T.: and, for the matter of that, her ladyship knows *my* address, having visited here.

'A sudden thought came over me. "My dear Mrs. Titmarsh," said I, "you know how poor and how good your husband is."

'"Yes," says she, rather surprised.

'"Well, my dear," says I, looking her hard in the face, "Lady Tiptoff, who knows him, wants a nurse for her son, Lord Poynings. Will you be a brave woman, and look for the place, and mayhap replace the little one that God has taken from you?"

'She began to tremble and blush; and then I told her what you, Mr. Sam, had told me the other day about your money matters; and no sooner did she hear it than she sprung to her bonnet, and said, "Come, come:" and in five minutes she had me by the arm, and we walked together to Grosvenor Square. The air did her no harm, Mr. Sam, and during the whole of the walk she never cried but once, and then it was at seeing a nursery-maid in the Square.

'A great fellow in livery opens the door, and says, "You're the forty-fifth as come about this 'ere place; but, fust, let me ask you a preliminary question. Are you a Hirishwoman?"

'"No, sir," says Mrs. T.

'"That's suffishnt, mem," says the gentleman in plush; "I see you're not by your axnt. Step this way, ladies, if you please. You'll find some more candidix for the place upstairs; but I sent away forty-four happlicants, because they *was* Hirish."

'We were taken upstairs over very soft carpets, and brought into a room, and told by an old lady who was there to speak very softly, for my lady was only two rooms off. And when I asked how the baby and her ladyship were, the old lady told me both were pretty well: only the doctor said Lady Tiptoff was too delicate to nurse any longer; and so it was considered necessary to have a wet-nurse.

'There was another young woman in the room – a tall, fine woman as ever you saw – that looked very angry and contempshious at Mrs. T. and me, and said, "I've brought a letter from the duchess whose daugher I nust; and I think, Mrs. Blenkinsop, mem, my Lady Tiptoff may look far before she finds such another nuss as me. Five feet six high, had the small-pox, married to a corporal in the Lifeguards, perfectly healthy, best of characties, only drink water; and as for the child, ma'am, if her ladyship had six, I've a plenty for them all."

'As the woman was making this speech, a little gentleman in black came in from the next room, treading as if on velvet. The woman got up, and made him a low curtsey, and folding her arms on her great broad chest, repeated the speech she had made before. Mrs. T. did not get up from her chair, but only made a sort of a bow; which, to be sure, I thought was ill manners, as this gentleman was evidently the apothecary. He looked hard at her and said, "Well, my good woman, and are you come about the place too?"

'"Yes, sir," says she, blushing.

'"You seem very delicate. How old is your child? How many have you had? What character have you?"

'Your wife didn't answer a word; so I stepped up, and said, "Sir," says I, "this lady has just lost her first child, and isn't used to look for places, being the daughter of a captain in the navy; so you'll excuse her want of manners in not getting up when you came in."

'The doctor at this sat down and began talking very kindly to her; he said he was afraid that her application would be unsuccessful, as Mrs. Horner came very strongly recommended from the Duchess of Doncaster, whose relative Lady Tiptoff was; and presently my lady appeared, looking very pretty, ma'am, in an elegant lace-cap and a sweet muslin *robe-de-sham*.

'A nurse came out of her ladyship's room with her; and while my lady was talking to us, walked up and down in the next room with something in her arms.

'First, my lady spoke to Mrs. Horner, and then to Mrs. T.; but all the while she was talking, Mrs. Titmarsh, rather rudely, as I thought, ma'am, was looking into the next room: looking – looking at the baby there with all her might. My lady asked her her name, and if she had any character; and as she did not speak, I spoke up for her, and said she was the wife of one of the best men in the world; that her ladyship knew the gentleman, too, and had brought him a haunch of venison. Then Lady Tiptoff looked up quite astonished, and I told the whole story: how you had been head clerk, and that rascal, Brough, had brought you to ruin. "Poor thing!" said my lady: Mrs. Titmarsh did not speak, but still kept looking at the baby; and the great big grenadier of a Mrs. Horner looked angrily at her.

'"Poor thing!" says my lady, taking Mrs. T.'s hand very kind, "she seems very young. How old are you, my dear?"

'"Five weeks and two days!" says your wife, sobbing.

'Mrs. Horner burst into a laugh; but there was a tear in my lady's eyes, for she knew what the poor thing was a-thinking of.

'"Silence, woman!" says she angrily to the great grenadier-woman, and at this moment the child in the next room began crying.

'As soon as your wife heard the noise, she sprung from her chair and made a step forward, and put both her hands to her breast and said, "The child – the child – give it me!" and then began to cry again.

'My lady looked at her for a moment, and then ran into the next room and brought her the baby; and the baby clung to her as if he knew her: and a pretty sight it was to see that dear woman with the child at her bosom.

'When my lady saw it, what do you think she did? After looking on it for a bit, she put her arms round your wife's neck and kissed her.

'"My dear," said she, "I am sure you are as good as you are pretty, and you shall keep the child: and I thank God for sending you to me!"

'"These were her very words; and Dr. Bland, who was standing by, says, "It's a second judgment of Solomon!"

'"I suppose, my lady, you don't want *me*?" says the big woman, with another curtsey.

'"Not in the least!" answers my lady, haughtily, and the grenadier left the room: and then I told all your story at full length, and Mrs. Blenkinsop kept me to tea, and I saw the beautiful room that Mrs. Titmarsh is to have next to Lady Tiptoff's; and when my Lord came home, what does he do but insist upon coming back with me here in a hackney-coach, as he said he must apologize to you for keeping your wife away.'

I could not help, in my own mind, connecting this strange event, which, in the midst of our sorrow, came to console us, and in our poverty to give us bread, – I could not help connecting it with the *diamond-pin,* fancying that the disappearance of that ornament had somehow brought a different and a better sort of luck into my family. And though some gents who read this, may call me a poor-spirited fellow for allowing my wife to go out to service, who was bred a lady and ought to have servants herself: yet, for my part, I confess I did not feel one minute's scruple or mortification on the subject. If you love a person, is it not a pleasure to feel obliged to him? And this, in consequence, I. felt. I was proud and happy at being able to think that my dear wife should be able to labour and earn bread for me, now misfortune had put it out of my power to support me and her. And now, instead of making any reflections of my own upon prison-discipline, I will recommend the reader to consult that admirable chapter in the life of Mr. Pickwick, in which the same theme is handled, and which shows how silly it is to deprive honest men of the means of labour just at the moment when they most want it. What could I do? There were one or two gents in the prison who could work (literary gents – one wrote his

'Travels in Mesopotamia,' and the other his 'Sketches at Almack's,' in the place); but all the occupation I could find was walking down Bridge Street, and then up Bridge Street, and staring at Alderman Waithman's windows, and then at the black man who swept the crossing. I never gave him anything; but I envied him his trade and his broom, and the money that continually fell into his old hat. But I was not allowed even to carry a broom.

Twice or thrice – for Lady Tiptoff did not wish her little boy often to breathe the air of such a close place as Salisbury Square – my dear Mary came in the thundering carriage to see me. They were merry meetings; and – if the truth must be told – twice, when nobody was by, I jumped into the carriage and had a drive with her; and when I had seen her home, jumped into another hackney-coach and drove back. But this was only twice; for the system was dangerous, and it might bring me into trouble, and it cost three shillings from Grosvenor Square to Ludgate Hill.

Here, meanwhile, my good mother kept me company; and what should we read of one day but the marriage of Mrs. Hoggarty and the Rev. Grimes Wapshot! My mother, who never loved Mrs. H., now said that she should repent all her life having allowed me to spend so much of my time with that odious, ungrateful woman; and added that she and I too were justly punished for worshipping the mammon of unright-eousness and forgetting our natural feelings for the sake of my aunt's paltry lucre. 'Well, Amen!' said I. 'This is the end of all our fine schemes! My aunt's money and my aunt's diamonds were the cause of my ruin, and now they are clear gone, thank heaven! and I hope the old lady will be happy; and I must say I don't envy the Rev. Grimes Wapshot.' So we put Mrs. Hoggarty out of our thoughts, and made ourselves as com-fortable as might be.

Rich and great people are slower in making Christians of their children than we poor ones, and little Lord Poynings was not christened until the month of June. A duke was one godfather, and Mr. Edmund Preston, the State Secretary, another; and that kind Lady Jane Preston, whom I have before spoken of, was the godmother to her nephew. She had not long been made acquainted with my wife's history; and both she and her sister loved her heartily and were very kind to her. Indeed, there was not a single soul in the house, high or low, but was fond of that good sweet creature; and the very footmen were as ready to serve her as they were their own mistress.

'I tell you what, sir,' says one of them. 'You see, Tit my boy, I'm a connyshure, and up to snough; and if ever I see a lady in my life, Mrs. Titmarsh is one. I can't be fimiliar with her – I've tried – ,'

'Have you, sir?' said I.

'Don't look so indignant! I can't, I say, be familiar with her as I am with you. There's a somethink in her, a jennysquaw, that haws me, sir! and even my lord's own man, that 'as 'ad as much success as any gentleman in Europe – he says that, cuss him – '

'Mr. Charles,' says I, 'tell my lord's own man that, if he wants to keep his place and his whole skin, he will never address a single word to that lady but such as a servant should utter in the presence of his mistress; and take notice that I am a gentleman, though a poor one, and will murder the first man who does her wrong!'

Mr. Charles only said 'Gammin!' to this: but psha! in bragging about my own spirit, I forgot to say what great good fortune my dear wife's conduct procured for me.

On the christening-day, Mr. Preston offered her first a five and then a twenty pound note; but she declined either: but she did not decline a present that the two ladies made her together, and this was no other than *my release from the Fleet*. Lord Tiptoff's lawyer paid every one of the bills against me, and that happy christening-day made me a free man. Ah! who shall tell the pleasure of that day, or the merry dinner we had in Mary's room at Lord Tiptoff's house, when my lord and my lady came upstairs to shake hands with me?

'I have been speaking to Mr. Preston,' says my lord, 'the gentleman with whom you had the memorable quarrel, and he has forgiven it, although he was in the wrong, and promises to do something for you. We are going down, meanwhile, to his house at Richmond; and be sure, Mr. Titmarsh, I will not fail to keep you in his mind.'

'*Mrs.* Titmarsh will do that,' says my lady; 'for Edmund is woefully smitten with her!' And Mary blushed and I laughed, and we were all very happy: and sure enough there came from

Richmond a letter to me, stating that I was appointed fourth clerk in the Tape and Sealing-wax Office, with a salary of 80*l*. per annum.

Here perhaps my story ought to stop; for I was happy at last, and have never since, thank heaven! known want: but Gus insists that I should add how I gave up the place in the Tape and Sealing-wax Office, and for what reason. That excellent Lady Jane Preston is long gone, and so is Mr. P – off in an apoplexy, and there is no harm now in telling the story.

The fact was, that Mr. Preston had fallen in love with Mary in a much more serious way than any of us imagined; for I do believe he invited his brother-in-law to Richmond for no other purpose than to pay court to his son's nurse. And one day, as I was coming post-haste to thank him for the place he had procured for me, being directed by Mr. Charles to the 'scrubbery,' as he called it, which led down to the river, – there, sure enough, I found Mr. Preston, on his knees too, on the gravel-walk, and before him Mary, holding the little lord.

'Dearest creature!' says Mr. Preston, 'do but listen to me, and I'll make your husband consul at Timbuctoo! He shall *never* know of it, I tell you: he *can* never know of it. I pledge you my word as a Cabinet Minister! Oh, don't look at me in that arch way! by heavens, your eyes kill me!'

Mary, when she saw me, burst out laughing, and ran down the lawn; my lord, making a huge crowing, too, and holding out his little fat hands. Mr. Preston, who was a heavy man, was slowly getting up, when, catching a sight of me looking as fierce as the crater of Mount Etna, – he gave a start back and lost his footing, and rolled over and over, walloping into the water at the garden's edge. It was not deep, and he came bubbling and snorting out again in as much fright as fury.

'You d—d ungrateful villain!' says he, 'what do you stand there laughing for?'

'I'm waiting your orders for Timbuctoo, sir,' says I, and laughed fit to die; and so did my Lord Tiptoff and his party, who joined us on the lawn: and Jeames the footman came forward and helped Mr. Preston out of the water.

'Oh, you old sinner!' says my lord, as his brother-in-law came up the slope. 'Will that heart of yours be always so susceptible, you romantic, apoplectic, immoral man?'

Mr. Preston went away, looking blue with rage, and ill-treated his wife for a whole month afterwards.

'At any rate,' says my lord, 'Titmarsh here has got a place through our friend's unhappy attachment; and Mrs. Titmarsh has only laughed at him, so there is no harm there. It's an ill wind that blows nobody good, you know.'

'Such a wind as that, my lord, with due respect to you, shall never do good to me. I have learned in the past few years what it is to make friends with the mammon of unrighteousness; and that out of such friendship no good comes in the end to honest men. It shall never be said that Sam Titmarsh got a place because a great man was in love with his wife; and were the situation ten times as valuable, I should blush every day I entered the office-doors in thinking of the base means by which my fortune was made. You have made me free, my lord; and thank God! I am willing to work. I can easily get a clerkship with the assistance of my friends; and with that and my wife's income, we can manage honestly to face the world.'

This rather long speech I made with some animation; for, look you, I was not over well pleased that his lordship should think me capable of speculating in any way on my wife's beauty.

My lord at first turned red, and looked rather angry; but at last he held out his hand and said. 'You are right, Titmarsh, and I am wrong; and let me tell you in confidence, that I think you are a very honest fellow. You sha'n't lose by your honesty, I promise you.'

Nor did I: for I am at this present moment Lord Tiptoff's steward and right-hand man: and am I not a happy father? and is not my wife loved and respected by all the country? and is not Gus Hoskins, my brother-in-law, partner with his excellent father in the leather way, and the delight of all his nephews and nieces for his tricks and fun?

As for Mr. Brough, that gentleman's history would fill a volume of itself. Since he vanished from the London world, he has become celebrated on the Continent, where he has acted a thousand parts, and met all sorts of changes of high and low fortune. One thing we may at least admire in the man, and that is, his undaunted courage; and I can't help thinking, as I have said before, that there must be some good in him, seeing the way in which his family are faithful to him. With respect to Roundhand, I had best also speak tenderly. The case of Roundhand *v.* Tidd is still in the memory of the public; nor can I ever understand how Bill Tidd, so poetic as he was, could ever take on with such a fat, odious, vulgar woman as Mrs. R., who was old enough to be his mother.

As soon as we were in prosperity, Mr. and Mrs. Grimes Wapshot made overtures to be reconciled to us; and Mr. Wapshot laid bare to me all the baseness of Mr. Smithers's conduct in the Brough transaction. Smithers had also endeavoured to pay his court to me, once when I went down to Somersetshire; but I cut his pretensions short, as I have shown. 'He it was,' said Mr. Wapshot, 'who induced Mrs. Grimes (Mrs. Hoggarty she was then) to purchase the West Diddlesex shares: receiving of course, a large bonus for himself. But directly he found that Mrs. Hoggarty had fallen into the hands of Mr. Brough, and that he should lose the income he made from the lawsuits with her tenants and from the management of her landed property, he determined to rescue her from that villain Brough, and came to town for the purpose. He also,' added Mr. Wapshot, 'vented his malignant slander against me; but heaven was pleased to frustrate his base schemes. In the proceedings consequent on Brough's bankruptcy, Mr. Smithers could not appear; for his own share in the transactions of the Company would have been most certainly shown up. During his absence from London, I became the husband – the happy husband of your aunt. But thought, my dear sir, I have been the means of bringing her to grace, I cannot disguise from you that Mrs. W. has faults which all my pastoral care has not enabled me to eradicate. She is close of her money, sir – very close; nor can I make that charitable use of her property which, as a clergyman, I ought to do; for she has tied up every shilling of it, and only allows me half-a-crown a week for pocket-money. In temper, too, she is very violent. During the first years of our union, I strove with her; yea, I chastised her; but her perseverance, I must confess, got the better of me. I make no more remonstrances, but am as a lamb in her hands, and she leads me whithersoever she pleases.'

Mr. Wapshot concluded his tale by borrowing half-a-crown from me, (it was at the Somerset Coffee-house in the Strand, where he came, in the year 1832, to wait upon me,) and I saw him go from thence into the gin-shop opposite, and come out of the gin-shop half-an-hour afterwards, reeling across the streets, and perfectly intoxicated.

He died next year: when his widow, who called herself Mrs. Hoggarty-Grimes-Wapshot, of Castle Hoggarty, said that over the grave of her saint all earthly resentments were forgotten, and proposed to come and live with us; paying us, of course, a handsome remuneration. But this offer my wife and I respectfully declined; and once more she altered her will, which once more she had made in our favour; called us ungrateful wretches and pampered menials, and left all her property to the Irish Hoggarties. But seeing my wife one day in a carriage with Lady Tiptoff, and hearing that we had been at the great ball at Tiptoff Castle, and that I had grown to be a rich man, she changed her mind again, sent for me on her death-bed, and left me the farms of Slopperton and Squashtail, with all her savings for fifteen years. Peace be to her soul! for certainly she left me a very pretty property.

Though I am no literary man myself, my cousin Michael (who generally, when he is short of coin, comes down and passes a few months with us) says that my Memoirs may be of some use to the public (meaning, I suspect, to himself); and if so, I am glad to serve him and them, and hereby take farewell: bidding all gents who peruse this, to be cautious of their money, if they have it; to be still more cautious of their friends' money; to remember that great profits imply great risks; and that the great shrewd capitalists of this country would not be content with four per cent for their money, if they could securely get more: above all, I entreat them never to embark in any speculation, of which the conduct is not perfectly clear to them, and of which the agents are not perfectly open and loyal.

ARNOLD BENNETT

HELEN WITH THE HIGH HAND

It is difficult to say who is the more delightful in this charming domestic comedy; James Ollerenshaw or high handed Helen who arrives to disturb his miserly, measured existence.

When Helen Rathbone met her estranged step-uncle James on a park bench in one of the Five Towns, no citizen of this provincial manufacturing region could have guessed what a turn events would take, least of all the two protagonists. Helen was quite convinced she could change James Ollerenshaw for the better, whilst he was equally determined that she should not. From that moment their lives were inextricably bound together and would affect many more inside and outside their circle.

JOSEPH CONRAD

WITHIN THE TIDES

Four tales from this modern master. *The Planter of Malata* is a man who does not count the cost to himself or others and his heart is set on Miss Moorsom. Cloete is *The Partner* of George Dunbar and an unscrupulous one at that. George needs money – lots of it.

The Inn of Two Witches is in Spain, but the story begins in a box of books bought in London, in a street which no longer exists. *Because of the Dollars* rounds off this quartet with a tale of the East; an exotic world peopled with characters like Captain Davidson. He used to smile a lot, but not any more . . . for there was very little to smile about on the night he ran his little steamer full of dollars into a jungle creek.

THOMAS HARDY
A CHANGED MAN

This collection contains, as well as the title story, *The Waiting Supper; Alicia's Diary; The Grave by the Handpost; Enter a Dragoon; A Tryst at an Ancient Earthwork; What the Shepherd Saw; A Committee-Man of 'The Terror'; Master John Horseleigh, Knight; The Duke's Reappearance;* and *The Romantic Adventures of a Milkmaid.*

Hardy's love of the eerie and the supernatural are brought out in full measure here. His skill at depicting topographical detail is also apparent, particularly in *A Changed Man* – set in Caster-bridge and instantly recognisable to readers famil-iar with that town. The story is that of a young hussar captain who resigns his commission to preach in a poor parish and, by so doing, causes his wife to leave him for another soldier. It is a fine portrait in a vivid set of stories guaranteed to delight all Hardy devotees.

ROBERT LOUIS STEVENSON

THE DYNAMITER

On the broad northern pavement of Leicester Square, three young men meet after years of separation. Concluding that the life of a detective is the only profession for a gentleman, the three separate to pursue their investigations.

The story moves from the pavements of London to frontier America, with its Mormon caravans and dark deeds at Salt Lake City, on to slavery and voodoo on a Caribbean island and back to London lodging houses and the secret underworld of anarchists and bomb plots. The book is dramatic, funny, exciting and always supremely readable.

ANTHONY TROLLOPE

THE VICAR OF BULLHAMPTON

Here is another of Trollope's splendid galleries of characters: Harry Gilmore, the Squire, Captain Walter Marrable, the Reverend Frank Fenwick and Mrs. Fenwick, who is as good a specimen of an English country parson's wife as you shall meet in any county – good-looking, fond of the society around her, with a little dash of fun, knowing in blankets and corduroys and coals and tea – knowing also in beer and gin and tobacco.

Between them, the Vicar of Bullhampton and his wife are acquainted with every man and woman in the parish, including the Balfours, Mary Lowther and the Brattles – the Brattles who live across the meadows at the old mill and who are to figure so prominently in this story, set in a quiet Wiltshire backwater.